'They...er...did some tests on me after the accident. Blood tests.'

He nodded, frowning. 'Go on.'

'They found something.'

His face filled with concern and she could imagine what he was thinking. A mass. A shadow. Some disease...

'What did they find?'

Emily searched his face, knowing the response he would give, knowing how his face would crumple at hearing the news, not sure if she could bear the way he would drop all contact with her, drop her hand that he was clutching so tight.

She'd missed *him*. So much!

But he'd made it clear he didn't want a baby with her. Telling him this was the hardest thing she would ever have to do.

'They found...' She paused, swallowing hard. 'I'm pregnant, Sam. I'm having our baby.'

Dear Reader,

Years ago, when my dad was in the army and stationed in Singapore, he overturned a water truck in the jungle and sustained a head injury. When he woke in hospital he had no idea of who he was or what had happened. The padre in the hospital found a love letter in his uniform pocket from my mum and he wrote to her, telling her what had happened and that she would need to help my father regain his memories—and make him fall in love with her all over again!

I always told my mum that she missed a trick in not 'reprogramming' my dad into a romantic Alpha hero! But, no, she did the right thing and told him the truth instead—even though my dad had sometimes been a naughty boy!

So I *had* to write an amnesia story for myself, and I really hope you will enjoy reading about Emily and Sam as they go on their own journey to find Sam's memories and restore their love.

Happy reading!

Louisa xxx

REUNITED BY THEIR PREGNANCY SURPRISE

BY
LOUISA HEATON

First published in Great Britain 2017
By Mills & Boon, an imprint of HarperCollins*Publishers*
1 London Bridge Street, London, SE1 9GF

Large Print edition 2017

ISBN: 978-0-263-06730-9

Our policy is to use papers that are natural, renewable and recyclable products and made from wood grown in sustainable forests. The logging and manufacturing processes conform to the legal environmental regulations of the country of origin.

Printed and bound in Great Britain
by CPI Antony Rowe, Chippenham, Wiltshire

Louisa Heaton lives on Hayling Island, Hampshire, with her husband, four children and a small zoo. She has worked in various roles in the health industry—most recently four years as a Community First Responder, answering 999 calls. When not writing, Louisa enjoys other creative pursuits, including reading, quilting and patchwork—usually instead of the things she *ought* to be doing!

Books by Louisa Heaton

Mills & Boon Medical Romance

The Baby That Changed Her Life
His Perfect Bride?
A Father This Christmas?
One Life-Changing Night
Seven Nights with Her Ex
Christmas with the Single Dad

Visit the Author Profile page
at millsandboon.co.uk for more titles.

For my mum and dad,
who had their own amnesia story.

Praise for
Louisa Heaton

'An emotional rollercoaster ride… *One Life-Changing Night* is medical drama at its best.'
—*Goodreads*

CHAPTER ONE

HER HEELS CLICK-CLACKED down the hospital corridor, a hurried, tense staccato, as Emily headed for the familiar room that Sam had been moved to after his short stay in the ICU.

She cut a striking figure in her stylish clothes, her long honey-blonde locks held back by sunglasses on her head and her large expensive bag swinging from the crook of her elbow. Her face, beautiful without the aid of make-up, was today showing strain. Lines and dark circles framed her eyes. And those who saw her noted the way her fingers twisted and fidgeted at her wedding band.

The Beverly West Hospital was the biggest and most prestigious hospital in Beverly Hills, Los Angeles, California. Sam's care here had been amazing. From the second he'd been scooped from their crumpled, steaming vehicle and blue-lighted to its doors, Emily had not doubted for one second the level of care they had both received. Apart from that split second when she'd first received her pregnancy test results…

Outside Sam's room she could see Dr Waters and her team, standing discussing something in low voices, with the occasional glance at Sam's notes on a clipboard. They looked serious. Concerned. But why? Hadn't they just rung her with the news that he was starting to wake up? That was *good*, right?

Dr Waters looked up as she became aware of Emily's approach and, meeting her by the door to the room, pasted a polite smile onto her face. 'Mrs Saint—'

'Is he awake?' She bit her lip and again twisted the wedding ring on her finger.

This was it. *Now or never.* She would go inside her husband's room and either find a man who was happy to be alive and willing to work on any problem, or the bear of a husband she'd been used to over the last few difficult months.

'He is. He's tired, and occasionally lapses back into sleep—which is normal considering the trauma his brain has been through. Coma patients usually take a day or two to wake properly.'

'I can go in and see him? Talk to him?'

The call from Dr Waters had come in the early hours of the morning. The phone ringing had not woken her. She'd already been awake. Lying in her very empty bed, staring at the ceiling and trying—still—to decide what was best to do.

Leave Sam? Or stay and fight for their marriage?

She'd even pulled a suitcase out and laid it on the bed one day, stood staring at it in numb indecision. Her heart wavering. It had all seemed so very clear-cut before the car crash. But now…? Knowing that he was sick…knowing that she was pregnant?

She had returned the suitcase to its storage spot and closed the doors on it. Her mind ran back to the times when Sam had refused to talk to her about having children, clamming up the second she raised it. Why had he done that? Over and over again? What hadn't he been telling her? There had to be something, but his refusal even to talk to her about it had been hurtful. They'd got to a point when they had barely been speaking to one another.

Her brain had almost torn itself in two, trying

to figure out his secret. Thinking of one scenario and then another. None had seemed likely, and she'd begun to believe that maybe he just didn't want to have a child with *her*.

Emily had stared at the closed closet doors, knowing that she would do what was *right*. And the right thing here was to give Sam time to recover and then let him know about the baby. Because then there was a small chance—a tiny, infinitesimal chance—that now the baby was no longer hypothetical but real and *here* he might change his mind.

She couldn't leave him without him knowing the truth. And if he heard the news about the pregnancy and *still* didn't want to be there for her and their child *then* she would go. Step out into the world on her own, even though doing so would break her heart. She didn't want to leave Sam, but he'd made life unbearable—had backed her into a corner.

Dr Waters shifted, looking at her colleagues, who all understood the implicit suggestion that perhaps they should leave, allow her to talk to Mrs Saint alone. They gave her sympathetic smiles and scurried away.

'Of course, but before you go in there's something you need to know.'

Her blood ran cold. Was there a problem? Brain injury? Dr Waters had mentioned that there might be the possibility of something like that once before. But Sam had recovered so quickly! His coma had been short, the ICP had dropped to normal levels incredibly quickly…

'What is it?'

Sam could have anything wrong. Be blind. Deaf. Find it difficult to talk or maybe swallow.

'We spoke once before about the damage that might have occurred to Sam's brain because of the injury to his head, and after a quick examination of your husband we believe that there seems to be some sort of memory deficit—mainly amnesia. It could be temporary, of course. He might remember everything after he's had another good sleep. But right now Sam seems… *confused* about his own timeline.'

Emily let out a long, slow, measured breath. Amnesia? She'd been fearing the worst! Temporary amnesia they could deal with.

'Is that all?'

Dr Waters frowned. 'Amnesia is a significant condition. I'm not sure you understand the full—'

'I'm going in to see him.' She cut off the doctor and stepped into Sam's room. She'd been waiting long enough for this moment. Ten long days. Nothing more could keep them apart.

Ten days. It had seemed like a lifetime.

Sometimes in those ten days she'd held his hand in hers, taking advantage of the fact that he was unconscious, remembering the happier times when they'd been close, pretending it was still that way. Sometimes she'd read to him from that day's newspaper, hoping that the sound of her voice would bring him back. And sometimes she'd just sat and stared at him, mulling everything over in her head, thinking of where they'd gone wrong and how she could fix it. Imagining the day he would wake—the day his eyelids would flutter open and he would see her, sitting by his bedside like a sentinel. How he would smile and say her name, reach out slowly for her hand and kiss her fingertips…

Okay, so maybe she lived in a fantasy land at times, but surely a touch of escapism had never hurt anyone.

'Sam?' So much hope, so much need was in the pitch of her voice.

Her husband lay in bed, his face pale and relaxed against pure white starched hospital pillows, his blue eyes slowly opening, wincing at the light in the room before fixing his gaze upon her.

And *smiling*!

It's been too long since you smiled at me like that...

It was like when they'd first been going out. The way he would look at her as if he was already in love with her. As if she was pure joy for him. Had no faults. Had not driven him crazy yet with endless requests to start a family. Okay, maybe not *crazy*, but she had tried to start that conversation lots of times. In the end even *she* had refused to talk. It had been too hard. Their conversations would always somehow end in arguments, and it had been easier just not to talk at all. She'd feared what would happen if they did.

Perhaps that had been a bad thing to do. Shutting down their communication. But she'd been trying to protect their relationship. She hadn't wanted it to end.

Sucking in a breath, she rushed to his side, dropping her bag on the floor, not caring as she reached for his outstretched hand, stooping down to kiss him, feeling his bristles scrape her face as his lips met hers. Nothing mattered at that moment apart from the fact that he was alive. Awake. Back with her. She never wanted to go through those ten days ever again.

It didn't matter that they'd been arguing. She was just happy that he was awake. Reacting. That he was looking at her and he was smiling and—

'How are you feeling?' She stroked his face, looking for clues, looking for any sign of discomfort that he might be trying to hide. Making sure that he wasn't in any pain. Her professional skills as a nurse-midwife were coming to the fore.

'Better for seeing you, Em,' he croaked, squeezing her fingers, and she looked down at their entwined hands and smiled.

All those days she had sat holding his hands and he had *never* squeezed back. Never shown any sign of life in his fingers. They'd just lain there, limp. Breaking her heart. It felt so good to be touching him again. Gaining strength from him.

'I've been so worried!' She sat on the bed facing him and ran her thumb over the backs of his hands.

He closed his eyes briefly, as if he couldn't stand the knowledge that she'd been so concerned for him. 'The doc says we've been in a car accident?'

The confusion in his face was heart-rending, but Emily guessed that this was the amnesia that Dr Waters had mentioned. Sam couldn't remember the crash. Sometimes people's brains would exclude certain bad experiences or memories, to help prevent itself from feeling hurt. Like a safety mechanism. If that was all that had happened to him then they'd both got away from this lightly.

'Yes.'

'Were *you* hurt?'

The concern in his voice and the way his blue eyes darkened at the thought relieved her. He *did* care for her! He *wasn't* angry at what had happened between them prior to this.

That was good, right? It took something like

this to wake people up. To make them notice what was important in life. *Each other.* They were stronger together than they were apart. Even if they *had* been disagreeing. Giving each other the cold shoulder.

'Not really. Just whiplash.'

He frowned. 'Whiplash can be serious, Em. Have you been checked out by the doctors?'

He reached up to stroke her face, then his hand fell to her shoulders and neck to rub at her muscles, but he must be feeling tired because his hand dropped back to the bed, his eyes closing as he drifted in and out of sleep, before opening them again.

'Look at me. Weak as a kitten.'

'You need to rest. You've been out of it for ten days.'

'Ten days?' He looked upset.

'They had to put you in an induced coma, Sam. Your brain got shook around in that hard skull of yours.'

He sighed and closed his eyes again and she realised with a sudden pang that he had drifted back to sleep. And she hadn't had a chance to tell him their news, yet.

It can wait. It's waited this long. What's a few more hours?

Right now he was happy to see her. Relieved. All signs of their previous turmoil was gone. They were speaking to each other. Something they hadn't done properly for weeks, and she'd missed that.

But it was odd, wasn't it? That he should be so happy to see her? After the last few days of stony silences, the weeks of arguing and disagreement…

She liked it that he was being nice. Concerned about her whiplash, concerned about *her* health, but she wasn't used to it. It was throwing her slightly.

Having to wait a little longer to deliver the news that she was pregnant was just fine. Because she had no idea how he would react to that. Probably not very well, and then they would be back to being at war with each other. She didn't mind holding off on that for a while.

She liked what they had right now, thank you very much. The talking. The concern for each other's wellbeing. The holding hands.

Emily stared at his hand in hers, lifted it to her

mouth and kissed it, inhaling the scent of him, breathing it in like vital oxygen. Then she got up off the bed and settled into her usual chair, staring long and hard at her husband.

She was getting him back. He'd smiled at her!

She felt sure there was a chance…all this just might be okay.

Sam slowly came to. He had a wicked headache, but he appeared to be still in hospital, attached to God only knew how many wires and monitors and, beside him, her head slumped to her shoulder, asleep, was his beautiful fiancée Emily.

She looked tired. Exhausted, even. Her face was a little pale beneath wave upon wave of that gorgeous hair of hers. But then he assumed she would be. Hadn't she, or someone, told him that he'd been out of it for ten days? After some accident he couldn't even recall?

Ten days. What had he missed? Probably nothing too much. That serial he'd been watching on television had been scheduled to show its last episode the other week, so probably that. There was still another month or so before Emily's birthday, so thankfully not that. He had a big surprise planned. He was hoping to take her to Las Vegas.

It was strange, though. Only ten days and he could swear that her hair seemed longer. A little more sun-bleached. Those honey tones were brighter than normal. And were those new clothes? He hadn't seen them before. But then again, Em did enjoy shopping. Perhaps she'd gone out and treated herself whilst she'd been waiting for him to recover? A little pick-me-up?

He lifted his head off the pillow to check himself out. There didn't appear to be any limbs wrapped in bandages, no plaster casts or anything like that. Had he just got a head injury? That would explain the headache, and the fact that he'd been out of it for a while. He hated it that he was laid up in hospital, because they still had so much to do. Not only did they need to tell everyone that Emily had accepted his proposal of marriage, but there was so much to do at work, too!

His idea, of building an exclusive five-star birth centre—the Monterey Birth Centre—was close to fruition. They'd toured the halls just last week and everything had looked perfect. Almost ready for their Grand Opening.

It was going to be massive. He wanted the Monterey to be the premier birthing centre in the whole of the US. He wanted people to aspire to have their babies there, to be treated as if they were royalty and enjoy the ultimate birthing experience, which he and his team would provide whilst their patients were being fed with delectable dishes provided by a team of Michelin-starred chefs in the kitchen.

It had taken a lot of planning. And sourcing funding. But he'd found people—mainly people whose babies he had already delivered safely—to sponsor and endorse the Monterey. He'd secured a great board of directors—along with himself and Emily, of course—and his excitement for this project had driven him onward like nothing he had ever experienced before. There'd been so much to think about! But he enjoyed that.

Asking Emily to marry him had been the icing on the cake. And she'd said yes. So he guessed now he'd be busy planning a wedding, too!

They hadn't been going out long. Six months? But there was something about her—something that had reached out and grabbed him. She'd seemed so…*vulnerable* when they'd first met, and he'd been cautious not to scare her with his desire to be by her side. He'd not been able to pinpoint the source of that vulnerability and, to be honest, they'd both been so busy at work, and setting up the Monterey, that it hadn't seemed all that important after a while.

Emily had blossomed by his side, driven on by their shared vision. She was everything he could have wished for and he loved her deeply. She cared for and loved delivering babies as much as he did.

But today she looked exhausted. She must have been handling any last hiccups at the birth centre, working *and* having to deal with his accident and their families all by herself. No wonder she looked shattered. Had they put off the Grand Opening whilst they'd waited for him to recover?

For a brief moment he just lay there and stared at her, his heart swelling with love for the woman at his side, but after a minute or so he couldn't stand it any more and reached out to take her hand. Needing to touch her. To connect.

She blinked herself awake in seconds. 'Sam?'

He smiled and lifted her hand to his lips, pressed a kiss upon it. 'Sleeping Beauty.'

She glanced at her watch in confusion. 'I've been asleep for three hours!' She rubbed at her eyes and then glanced at him with concern. 'How are you? Are you in any pain?'

'Just a headache.'

'Should I call a nurse?'

'No, it's fine. It's understandable, considering my head got bashed. I'm sure there's some morphine being dripped in to me somewhere…' He looked up at the various drips and then smiled at her. 'I've missed you.' He squeezed her fingers, wishing he could be holding her in his arms. Wishing he could get her to come and lie beside him upon the bed. He needed to feel her next to him.

She looked a little apprehensive. 'You've been in a coma.'

'So you keep saying. But what about *you*? How

are you doing? Any problems with Monterey I need to know about?'

Emily frowned and shook her head. 'No. It's all going very well.'

He let out a sigh. 'That's great news. How did Harry get on with the window treatments? Did he make the changes we asked him to?'

His fiancée looked at him, lines furrowing her brow. 'What?'

'The curtains and sashing in The Nightingale Suite. We decided to change them to that lighter gold colour. Has he done it yet? If he hasn't we need to get on that—the Grand Opening is only a few days away.'

She continued to look at him with puzzlement. 'What are you talking about?'

'The curtains were too dark. That suite is going to be our most prestigious—we want it right for the press tour. Think of the spread of pictures…'

'Press tour? We haven't had a press tour since…' Her voice drifted away and she suddenly looked at him, her eyes searching his face as she sucked in a breath. 'Sam, what day do you think it is?'

He closed his eyes and thought about it. He'd proposed on Friday, he'd been in a coma for ten days, so today had to be… 'Monday? Tuesday, maybe?'

She shook her head, her choppy blonde locks shimmering around her shoulders. 'No. I mean the month. The *year*.'

Month and year? What was she talking about? He'd been out for ten days, they'd said! He told her the date and watched as what little colour there was leeched from her face. She turned away from him, her curtain of honey-blonde hair hiding her face from his as she pulled her hands free of his grasp.

Her recoiling from him made him feel nervous. What didn't he know? 'Why are you asking? I'm not that much out of step, am I?'

He heard her sniff. Watched as she reached into her bag and pulled out a small hankie, dabbing at her eyes before she turned back to face him, bracing herself to prepare to say something she clearly thought he wouldn't be ready to hear.

'Sam… We've been married for *eighteen months*. The Monterey has been open and running for just over a year now.'

Sam stared at her hard. He swallowed painfully and his hands scrunched up the bedding as he made fists.

Eighteen months?

No! That's ridiculous…

'Why would you say that? Why would you even play a trick like that?'

A tear dripped onto her cheek and with clear-cut pain in her voice she said, 'I'm not lying to you.'

'Emily…'

'Sam, please, listen—'

But he wasn't listening. Not any more. Em was playing some cruel trick on him, and he didn't know why, but the doctors would have to tell him the truth! The nurses would. He'd make them show him a newspaper or something. This was completely ridiculous. There was *no way* that he'd lost all that time. He'd *know*. There'd be signs!

Sam stabbed at the button that would call a nurse to his bedside and kept doing so, ignoring Emily's pleas, her cries. She was standing now, her hand covering her mouth, looking at him with those wide, tear-filled eyes…

The door opened and a nurse he hadn't seen before came in. She glanced at Emily in concern before turning to him. 'Mr Saint?'

'I need to see the doctor in charge of my care.'

The nurse kept on looking between the two of them, not sure exactly what had happened. 'Dr Waters has gone home for the evening. I can get—'

'Get *someone*! Someone who knows what they're talking about!' He glared at Emily, angry at her, and watched as she snatched up her handbag and ran from the room.

The nurse nodded and hurried out, and with both women gone he felt his anger deflate slightly.

Married eighteen months? Emily was crazy. Perhaps *she'd* had the bump on the head and not him!

He lay in the bed, fury surging through him,

and waited for someone who knew what they were talking about to come and tell him the truth.

There was no way he had lost *that* amount of time.

CHAPTER TWO

EMILY RAN FROM Sam's room, throwing her bag to the floor and sagging against the wall opposite. She slid down it until she sat hunched on the floor, like a puppet without her strings.

He couldn't remember! He had no idea of how much time had passed! He thought…he thought that… She heard his words once again, spoken with such certainty, such concern. *'How did Harry get on with the window treatments? Did he make the changes we asked him to?'*

Window treatments?

I remember! It was a week before the Grand Opening. He'd proposed just the night before...

The nurse who had followed her out of Sam's room came over to her, hunched down and draped her arm softly around her shoulders. 'Are you okay, Mrs Saint?'

She could barely breathe…so, no, she wasn't okay. But she managed to suck in a deep, steadying breath and struggle back to her feet. Another breath and she nodded that she was all right.

'The doctor told me… Dr Waters…she told me that Sam had a little amnesia, but I thought that she meant that…that he'd forgotten the *accident.* Not two whole years of his *life*!'

It was so much for her to take in. And she couldn't imagine how *he* felt! Well, she didn't have to, did she? He was furious at the idea. And she could understand why. Sam was a driven man, always pushing himself to fill every second of his life and enjoy it. The man didn't sit still for a minute.

And he'd forgotten it all. The opening of the birth centre. The massive celebrations…the parties. The first birth and all the births since. The amazing write-ups they'd received, the recommendations, the people who were attracted to the Monterey—celebrities, the rich… *Royalty* had even given birth there.

And not just everything that had happened at work. If it were true—if he really didn't remember—then he'd also forgotten their wedding. The preparations, the wedding night, the honeymoon in Paris…

The arguments... The fact that I told him I was going to leave him!

Emily bit down hard on her lip and accepted a plastic cup of water from the nurse, who had hurried to the small self-service station in the corridor. 'Thank you.'

'I'll page the on-call doctor.'

Emily nodded. 'Thank you.' She smiled weakly at the nurse, noting the relief on her face, her name badge—Melanie. 'And I think you'd better show him a webpage, or perhaps a newspaper. Prove the date to him. I'm not sure he believes me.'

Melanie looked uncertain. 'I think maybe the doctor ought to do that.'

'Maybe. Or perhaps I ought to do it? Do you have a copy of today's paper?'

Not that she *wanted* to go in there and do that to him. *Prove* to him that all that she'd said was true. That he was a man out of time with everyone else.

How did you get your head around something like that?

'I'd like whoever's on call to talk to both of us. I need to know what this means. Why it's happened. What we should be doing…' Her thoughts drifted off onto some nightmarish plane where Sam *never* regained those two years and she had to fill him in on *everything*. The long hours he'd put in, his absences from home, the arguments…

And somehow I need to tell him I'm pregnant too!

She felt sick. The weight of all this duty pressed down upon her. A thick ball of nausea sat low and curdled in her stomach and she could taste bile in the back of her throat, despite the drink of cool, refreshing water from the cup. Was there an easy way to tell a man that you were married, but that the two of you had been arguing constantly and that just under two weeks ago you'd told that same man you were going to leave him?

Because you refused to have a child with me and, oh, by the way, I'm actually pregnant! I found out after the accident. They did tests.

Yes, she really couldn't see that nugget of information going down very well with him.

It was all going wrong. Everything.

She tried to rack her brains for what she knew about amnesia, but apart from the general knowledge that it meant you couldn't remember things, she wasn't sure what else she knew about it. It wasn't something she'd specialised in. She was a certified nurse-midwife. She looked after labouring women.

She knew that there were different types of amnesia—some amnesia was permanent and some temporary. Dr Waters had said it might be so. If Sam's was temporary then he would regain his memories on his own and everything would be back to the way it was before…

But I was leaving him before.

She swallowed hard, seeing in her mind's eye that day she'd laid the suitcase upon the bed and stared at it. Then she'd lain a hand on her abdomen. This wasn't just about her and Sam any more. There was a baby to consider, and there was no way she was going to let her child be rejected by its father before it was even born. She knew what it felt like to be left behind and unwanted. It hurt. Left you bewildered. Made you question yourself. Your own value. She would not put her own child through that.

Emily swallowed the last of the water and crumpled the plastic cup. She put it into a trash can and walked back over to Sam's door, put her hand on it, waiting, taking a deep breath.

She was about to go back in when Melanie reappeared.

'I have a paper for you.'

She looked down. Saw the day's headlines. The date. 'Thank you.' Her mouth felt dry. There was a strange, tinny sort of taste in her mouth and she wondered if she were going to be sick.

'And the doctor will come down as soon as he's finished with a patient on the next floor. Ten minutes?'

Emily nodded, swallowing hard. 'Brilliant. Thanks.'

She watched as Melanie headed back to answer a ringing telephone and then with one final inhalation she pushed open Sam's door and stepped inside.

Their gazes met across the room.

If I'm going to get through this then I need to be strong.

'I've brought you something.'

'An apology?' He sounded bitter. Hurt.

'No. I don't need to give you one. But I will give you this.' She walked across the room and handed him the newspaper before stepping back. As if imagining that the second he confirmed the date for himself he would somehow explode. 'Look at the date.'

At first she didn't think he would look at it, but he finally lifted the paper and scanned the first page for the date.

She knew the exact second his gaze fell upon it. He seemed to stiffen, the muscle in his jaw flickering, the focus in his eyes intensifying before he flipped through, checking that all the other pages stated the same date, too. Then he went back to the beginning, scanned the headlines.

Sam dropped the paper as if it were contaminated, closing his eyes briefly as it all sank in.

'Two years? I've lost *two years*?'

He sounded so broken. So *hurt*. It made her heart ache. Made her feel like she needed to cross the room to him and take him in her arms and hug him better. She didn't want him to be hurting. She never had.

'I'm so sorry, Sam. But it's true. We've been married eighteen months now. We honeymooned in Paris. We were very happy.'

He instantly looked up, met her gaze, pinning her with his normally soft blue eyes. *'Were?'*

She tried not to cry. She seemed to be so emotional since finding out she was pregnant. She struggled to keep control of her voice. 'We're having one or two…problems.'

Sam bristled. 'What kind of problems?'

Emily shook her head. 'We can talk about those later. The doctor's coming to talk to you now. About the amnesia.'

'Are there problems at work? Is the Monterey *failing*?'

She could hear the fear in his voice. The concern. 'No. It's doing very well. The launch was amazing and we've had almost full capacity from day one. You haven't stopped working—working all hours to make it a success.'

At that moment the door opened and a new doctor came in, holding Sam's case notes in his hands.

Emily snapped to attention and crossed her arms, stepping back out of the doctor's way.

'Mr and Mrs Saint? I'm Dr Elijah Penn—how can I be of assistance?'

She managed a weak smile and went over to

shake Dr Penn's hand. 'Hello, Doctor. My husband has just learned that he's lost two years of his memory after his head injury. We were in a car crash together ten days ago. We were wondering if you could tell us some more about what to expect, and what we can do to help him regain his memory.'

Dr Penn frowned. 'I've only had a brief read-through of your notes, Mr Saint, and without giving you a thorough examination and questioning you myself over what you remember I can't be precise here. There are many different types of amnesia caused by traumatic head injury and right now it would be hard to be specific.'

'Can you tell us what you *do* know?'

'I wouldn't like to guess, as I'm not your husband's physician and I wouldn't want to tell you anything erroneous. But if you'll give me a moment or two with your husband then I'll tell you what I can.'

Emily nodded. Okay. That sounded sensible. She left Sam's room once again and went and sat outside. From her purse she pulled out her cell phone and felt drawn to the photo album.

Opening it, she began flicking through. Perhaps there was something here that might help Sam? Perhaps if he looked at their moments together that might provoke some kind of memory?

There were lots to go through. Many of the photographs were from work. Mothers-to-be whom she'd become great friends with, bouquets that she'd been sent as thanks. There were some pictures of the house after they'd had some work done on it. Other people's babies.

Why weren't there any pictures of her and Sam *together*? She had a few selfies. One or two of Sam in scrubs about to go into a Caesarean section, and then one of him relaxing at the house, reading a work journal. In neither of them was he smiling that beautiful smile she hadn't seen for such a long time. When had he last smiled at her? Apart from today? Because that didn't count any more, did it? He was of the mind-set that she'd just accepted his proposal. He thought they were *happy*.

If only...

She scrolled furiously through the rest of the photos. Nothing of them together except for one right at the beginning, when she'd first got the phone, of her and Sam, heads together, smiling at the camera.

When had that been? She checked the date stamp. It had been just after the Monterey had opened. Of course they'd been happy then. Work had been enthralling. They'd been busy. Passing like ships in the night, sometimes, but planning their wedding.

She felt the tears threaten once again and stood up abruptly, shaking them off. What on earth was she going to do? And how was Sam feeling? Thinking they were blissfully happy only to learn that he couldn't remember his own wedding and had no idea that over the last eighteen months he had slowly been distancing himself from her.

The doctor came to the door. 'Would you like to come in?'

Emily shoved the phone back in her jacket pocket and hurried through, glancing at Sam. He looked glum, but reached out his hand.

Puzzled, but hopeful, she went over to him and took his hand in hers, her heart pounding in her chest because he'd reached out to her. Needed her. He hadn't done that for such a long time.

'Bad news?'

Dr Penn held his clipboard against his chest. 'I've had a chance to chat with your husband. Ask him a few questions. See what he understands of his situation. You've both been very lucky in that you escaped the car accident with a minimum amount of injuries. But from my understanding from this limited examination I would presume to say that Sam is suffering from a retrograde amnesia.'

Emily squeezed his fingers and looked at him. 'Which is...?'

'It can be caused by various conditions including head trauma, which Sam has gone through. Retrograde amnesia means that Sam's most recent memories are less likely to be recalled, but his long-term memories are easier for him to remember.'

'Right.'

'It's usually temporary, which is the good thing—though I have to warn you, of course, that not everyone will experience it that way. Sam may be unlucky. We have no way of knowing for sure into which camp Sam will fall.'

'But if it is temporary…is there anything we can do to try and help the memories come back?'

Dr Penn nodded. 'It can help to try and provoke those memories. Show Sam familiar things—photos, videos, possessions, favourite foods, smells, clothing. Anything and everything that might help the memories come back.'

'Places? Like if I took him to where we got married or our favourite restaurant?'

'Anywhere he can be immersed for as long as possible should help. Usually it's not just one item that makes memories return but a drowning in overall sensation—place, aroma, sounds, people. All of it at once. Like déjà-vu.'

Sam spoke up. 'So if I went home…that might do it?'

'It could, but I can't promise anything. Memories can take days or even weeks to return.' He swallowed. 'Maybe longer.'

'And would they all come back straight away?'

'It's different for everyone.'

Sam squeezed her hand. 'So can I go home?'

Dr Penn shook his head. 'Not straight away. I know you didn't suffer any broken bones or organ damage, but you did have a nasty hit to the head and you had a stent fitted to drain fluid. We need to monitor you for a while yet, and if you manage to stay stable, with no spikes of temperature or complications, and physio goes well, then maybe we'll look at letting you go.' He smiled. 'Now, if you'll excuse me, I have another patient to attend to.'

They watched the doctor disappear and Emily turned to Sam, aware that they were still holding hands. It was nice. It had been a long time since he had held her like that and she hated how much she needed his touch to reassure her. She didn't want to let him go. She never had.

'How are you feeling, Sam? After all that?'

'It's a lot to take in. But I guess I ought to look on the bright side.'

She frowned. 'Bright side?'

He nodded. 'Yes. I know who I am. I know who you are. I still have all the knowledge that lets me be an OB/GYN. I can still work—eventually.' He waited until she looked him fully in the eyes. 'I know how much I love you.'

She swallowed and smiled, trying to still the beating of her heart. It was running away with joy at his words. For how long had she yearned to hear those simple words from Sam?

But there's still so much you don't know!

Could she truly revel in those three simple words? He'd said he loved her, but he still didn't know the truth of their marriage.

He'd hurt her. She'd felt so rejected, so forgotten as Sam had stayed at work, or gone to fundraising galas without her, or disappeared to play tennis with his lawyer. All those arguments they'd had…all those harsh words they'd said to each other out of spite or desperation. How could she forget all they had gone through?

He had. Completely. Right now he was unaware of it all.

But she…? She remembered it all too well. Every argument was a scar upon her heart.

He was trying to be positive. She could see that. *Feel* that. Should she burst his bubble now? Tell him about the baby?

He needed to know. Needed to hear the truth so that he could be in full possession of the facts. The facts he needed, anyway.

'There's something more, Sam.'

'Oh?'

'You're not going to like it.'

He smiled. 'Let me be the judge of that.'

His smile twanged her heartstrings. It was so familiar! Held so much of that gorgeous cheeky charm that she'd fallen in love with!

But she knew. Knew Sam didn't want a baby. He wasn't ready for one after being married for *eighteen months.* Why would he feel ready for one when he'd thought they weren't even married?

'They…did some tests on me after the accident. Blood tests.'

He nodded, frowning. 'Go on.'

'They found something.'

His face filled with concern and she could imagine what he was thinking. Cancer. A mass. A shadow. Some disease…

'What did they find?'

She searched his face, knowing the response he would give, knowing how his face would crumple at hearing the news, not sure if she could bear the way he would drop all contact with her, let go of the hand that he was clutching so tight. Be angry with her again just as she'd started to enjoy the way he held her hand, the way he'd smiled at her before he started to learn the truth.

She'd missed *him*. So much!

But he'd made it clear he didn't want a baby with her, so telling him this was the hardest thing she would ever have to do. It might end them. But she had no choice.

'They found…' She paused, swallowing hard, 'I'm pregnant, Sam. I'm having our baby.'

He knew he was staring at her, but he couldn't stop. She was…*pregnant*?

Images of Serena instantly flooded his brain and he blinked them away. *No.* He would not think of her. That was all too raw, still. Because even though many years had passed he'd pushed away what had happened and stamped it down low.

Pregnant. *Pregnant!* Emily. His fiancée. No. That was wrong—Emily was now apparently his wife. For almost two years. And she was having a—

He swallowed hard.

He loved this woman. He loved her so much! He should be pleased. But the way she was looking at him right now… Like she was *frightened* of his response? Like she was expecting him to start stamping around the room, or throwing things, or—

Sam knew what he ought to do. He should smile, say that it was *great news*, pretend that he was thrilled, but…

I'm going to be a father. I'm going to be...a father!

Surely she knew how he felt about this? What had happened to Serena had almost destroyed him. How had they been so careless?

Tentacles of fear wrapped themselves around him and tried to suck him down into that deep, dark well of pain he'd kept hidden for so long. Having that kind of responsibility, having to be the one to take care of a young baby every day, was just so…

His heart thudded in his chest so loudly he thought he could hear it in his ears. His skin grew hot, clammy, and he could feel the beginning of the shakes. *My body...it's surging with adrenaline...* The last time he'd felt this way had been after they'd found Serena…

Sam blinked slowly. Emily was still waiting

for his reaction, and though the idea of becoming a father terrified him he loved her so much he just knew he couldn't let her see it. Couldn't let her see his inadequacies. Couldn't let her see his Achilles' heel. She would think him an absolute monster if he started on her about this, and both of them had been through too much just lately. His true reaction would have to wait. Maybe when he was out of hospital they could talk sensibly about this.

So he managed to let out a breath and grasped her fingers tightly. 'You're pregnant? Emily… that's so…' he forced the word, trying to make it sound authentic *'…amazing!'*

And he pulled her into his arms and clasped her tightly, breathing in the delicious scent of her honey hair and closing his eyes with such intense pain in his heart, hoping that she could not sense his betrayal.

He felt her relax and sink into him, gasping with relief.

'You mean it? You're happy?' Emily pulled back to search his face, her own riddled with tears, unable to believe that this was true. But true it was. Because Sam was nodding and smiling and happy. And somehow *this* Sam—this version of Sam who had believed it was two years earlier and they were newly engaged—seemed *happy* at the idea of becoming a father!

And if he's happy then...maybe we can be happy too?

She kissed his face without thinking, clutching it with hands that were trembling. She'd been about to *leave* him! She'd almost packed her things. Had written him that letter. They'd crashed their car arguing over this. It was unbelievable.

His reaction, though welcome, was startling. Now the relief of telling him about the baby had passed without bad incident she began to feel pangs of doubt.

'Of course I mean it. How could I not?' He swallowed. 'How far along are you?' he asked, with real curiosity.

She smiled, almost shyly, amazed that she was getting to talk to him about this. Normally! Without him throwing a fit and storming out! 'About nine weeks, I think.'

'Nine weeks…' He looked up at her and smiled

broadly once again. 'Still in the first trimester? I guess we really ought not to tell anyone yet.'

'You could tell your family if you want to.'

Sam shook his head. 'No, I… I think it's best we wait until you're in the fourth month.'

'Okay. Whatever you think is best. I'm so glad you're happy about this. I thought—'

'Thought what?'

She shook her head, as if her answer had been too silly to contemplate. 'It doesn't matter.'

This truly was an opportunity, Emily thought, for them to save their marriage. Sam loved her. He seemed happy to be a father. Was there any need to tell him what their relationship had really been like? This might be a chance for Emily to wipe their slates clean and start again.

Although it wouldn't be a totally fresh start. Because for her the upset of the last few weeks and months was still there. Just because Sam didn't know, it didn't mean that she'd forget too. But it might be a start. A way to save them, built on who they had been in the beginning of their relationship. In love. Supporting each other's hopes and dreams. There had been no need for her to get the suitcase out of the closet.

And what harm could it do? They'd nearly separated, but now...? Now things seemed to have changed. Sam seemed happy about the baby, despite everything, and that was what she'd wanted the most. She'd been granted her wish—only a fool would throw it all away now. She'd been desperate before, when she'd been on the verge of leaving him. But now she was being presented with a second chance.

And, yes, his memories might come back to him and cause them problems later, but what if they *didn't*? And if they did—well, Sam was happy to be a dad right now. If they both worked really hard on their relationship, then surely all that was in the past...could be washed under the bridge?

This was a second chance for them, and for the sake of their unborn baby Emily was prepared to risk it.

She'd always fought for their marriage. Had tried everything to save it. What was one last secret?

* * *

The second Emily left his hospital room to head home for the night Sam slumped back against his pillows, exhausted.

A baby...

It was such a huge responsibility. For years. A lifetime. And the weight of that responsibility was not something he thought he could bear.

What had he been thinking, getting Emily pregnant? Had they not been using protection? How had he allowed himself this colossal mistake?

He couldn't be a good father. Hadn't he proved himself incapable of looking after a baby? That was why being an OB/GYN was so beautiful. He could keep babies safe at work. Get them through their nine months of gestation as safely and healthily as possible and then make sure that the mother delivered her child without problems.

At the hospital he had a team. He was supported. He had the most recent advancements, tests and medications at his fingertips. Was able to experience joy with the family as he brought new life into the world. Holding a newborn baby...there was nothing in the world like it. It was a privilege. Magical. A brand-new person and he would be the first one to hold it, before he delivered it into the hands of its parents. The elation, the thrill in the room could not be surpassed. And then, once the umbilical cord was clamped and cut, Sam's job—Sam's *responsibility*—was over. He could relax. Let go.

Sam loved delivering babies. Hadn't he wanted to do that for so long? Hadn't he delighted in the miracle of birth so much he had made it his vocation? Deciding that because he hadn't been able to save Serena he could save others?

But after the birth?

No. That was when it could all go wrong. It was why he'd interviewed and hired the best, most elite team of neonatologists and paediatricians for aftercare at his Monterey centre.

He'd vowed *never* to put himself in that position again, and when he'd first met Emily he'd thought he'd found someone just like him. Someone who loved delivering babies but who didn't want one of their own.

Wasn't that what she'd said? Early on? He felt sure that she had. He had a blurry recollection of it.

They'd met in a delivery room. Their eyes meeting across a crowded stirrup. Em had been working as a private midwife and had brought in a couple whose home birth plan had gone awry. As the OB/GYN on call, he'd gone to the room to assist with a Ventouse delivery and had been physically struck by the sight of her beside her patient, clutching the mother's hand through each contraction, coaching her, intently focused on her.

He recalled a brief moment of wondering who this beautiful new midwife was before he'd got to work, and once the baby had arrived—safely, of course—he had left the room. Only for her to follow him outside and thank him.

I stared at her.

He smiled at the memory. He'd literally been struck dumb. Unable to speak. Her blonde hair had been messy, her cheeks rosy, and she'd been wearing these crazy dangly earrings with turquoise stones that almost matched her eyes. And she'd been wearing flats, so she'd seemed only as tall as his shoulders, and he could remember thinking that she was like an elf.

Eventually he'd managed to get his tongue and

mouth to form simple words. 'You did a great job in there.'

'Me? No, it was nothing to do with me. You did all the work.'

'Well, it's my job.'

'Yes.' She'd stared back at him as if she'd been trying to work something out in her head. 'I love having babies.'

He'd frowned. 'You have children of your own?'

She'd shaken her head, as if realising she'd said something that she shouldn't. 'No! God, no! I don't want any yet.'

He'd smiled, intrigued. He'd wanted to know more about her. Wanted to see her.

His only focus had been to be with her. To soak her up. They'd had such fun together, shared so many likes and opinions.

It had been easy to get carried away in the whirlwind.

CHAPTER THREE

THE NEXT DAY a young man called Matt came to Sam's room to help him 'mobilise'. He was in the middle of trying not to feel too dizzy and light-headed after standing up for the first time when Emily came into his room.

His heart soared at seeing her, despite all his dark thoughts the previous night. She looked fresh and bright, a bohemian chic angel, as if she'd had a really good night's sleep, and she developed a huge smile on her face when she saw him standing up, holding onto a walker.

'You're up!'

'Not for long.' Sam collapsed down onto the bed and let out a heavy breath, clutching his head as if to steady it.

Matt cocked his head to one side. 'Dizzy?'

'Yeah, a little.'

'It'll pass if you take it easy. Try this: whilst you're sitting down, really push your feet into the floor and flex and release your calf muscles. It'll help pump the blood around your system and prevent a blood pressure drop next time you stand.'

Emily stood by his side and hesitantly laid a supportive hand upon his shoulder. She smelt minty fresh and was wearing a perfume he didn't recognise, but liked.

He looked up at her, expecting her to kiss him hello, but she didn't. Because of Matt's presence? It seemed unlikely. But now that she was here he wanted to show her what he could do. Show her that he was going to get stronger every day. He wanted to be back on his feet. He wanted to be up and about again. Working. Being Sam. He hated being stuck in a hospital bed.

Gripping the walker once again, Sam stood. Slower this time. He took a moment to make sure the dizziness wasn't about to make him collapse onto the floor and then pushed the walker to one side and took a step forward. Matt stood close, ready to steady him if needed.

Who knew lying on your back for ten days after a head injury would make you feel as weak as a baby bird? After just a few steps he was ready to sit down, but Sam was determined to push through. He kept going. Made it across the room, out of the door to the nurses' station and back again. By the time he got back to his bed he was exhausted, sweating as if he'd just done a full day's training in the gym, and he sank back onto the mattress with a broad grin on his face.

Matt smiled. 'So…you're one of *those* people.'

Sam raised an eyebrow in question.

'Type A. High achiever. It's good, but you also need to know when to stop.'

Emily sat beside him on the bed and passed him a towel to freshen up with. 'He's always pushed himself and strived for the best.'

'Yes, well, just keep an eye on that blood pressure. It won't always be as low as it was about five minutes ago.'

'I'm fine, Matt. Honestly. I won't stop pushing until I'm in my own home.'

Matt nodded. 'And probably not even then. I'll come back later, after your evening meal, and we'll do some more. In the meantime, rest. You're allowed to get up to use the bathroom only.' Matt saluted him and walked away.

Emily peered into his eyes. 'Do you remember home?'

Sam looked at her, tempted just to ignore the question and kiss her. Having her this close to him, smelling as good as she did, looking as beautiful as she did…

He reached up and tucked a strand of her choppy blonde hair behind her ear. 'Are we still in the apartment? The two-bedroom place with the sliding doors out onto the balcony? View across the city?'

He could picture that quite clearly. It wasn't a problem. He very much wanted to get back there.

But the slump in Emily's shoulders informed him that it wasn't the right answer. 'No. We don't live there any more.'

Sam tried to think hard. To force memories to the surface. But he couldn't. It was as if there was a thick wall in his head, blocking them, and no matter how hard he pounded against it, no matter how ferociously he yelled at it and fought to knock it down, it resolutely remained.

'Then where?'

'We have a house in Beverly Hills now. You found it for us. It's white. Very neo-classical—

columns, balconies, topiaries, big doors…that sort of thing.'

He tried to imagine it, but was more concerned with the way she'd described it. 'You don't seem to like it.'

'I do. It's just…' She paused for a moment, looking down at the cover on his bed and straightening out a ripple on the surface. 'I guess we haven't made it *ours* yet.' She smiled weakly, but then stood up and tried to become more up-beat. 'But look at you! Only woke yesterday and already you're pounding the floors of the hospital!'

He could tell she wasn't telling him everything. Did she not like their home? Was it a place that *he'd* liked and pushed her into buying? There was *something*...

But he dismissed it quickly as he thought of his triumph without the walker and stood up again, pulling her into his arms, searching her gorgeous blue-green eyes for that quirky happy girl he knew so well.

'I've missed you.'

She wrapped her arms around his waist hesitantly, as if it was something she hadn't done in a long time, as if she was trying not to make it seem like she was pulling away.

But why would that be? They'd only been married a short time—surely they were still very physical?

'Kiss me.'

'*Sam!* The physio said you should be resting. You need to get back into bed!'

'And I will! But only if my wife joins me.' Sam tilted her chin up and showed her a cheeky grin before he brought his lips to hers.

The last time he'd kissed her had been… Well, just after she'd accepted his proposal. In *his* mind, anyway. And he was still full of that celebratory need to show her how much he loved her, despite all that had happened—the car crash, the pregnancy, the head injury, the amnesia. As far as he knew he'd only just slipped that ring onto her finger and he was feeling full to the brim with happiness.

However…

They were *married*. And expecting a baby. So surely they had to be getting along. And, despite his trepidation, his fears and his doubts, there was one thing clear in his mind. His love for Emily. And right now he felt that he needed her. The last few hours had been a lot to take in. To believe he had lost two whole years of his life was…mind-blowing. His pet project—his dream—the Monterey Birth Centre had opened and begun trading all without his knowledge.

Okay, so *technically* he'd been there. He'd orchestrated it, arranged it, even shown up to work there, apparently, but that was just what Emily had *told* him had happened. As far as he was concerned it still *hadn't* happened, and whilst he was stuck in this hospital life would continue to carry on without him. He needed to get home. Needed to see the Monterey in action. Needed to think about how he and Emily would tackle their new challenges.

He pulled back and looked into his wife's eyes. 'I can't wait to get home.'

She seemed breathless, her eyes glazed. 'Me too.'

It took two weeks before the hospital was even prepared to *consider* releasing Sam. In that time he received lots of welcome visitors—Emily, his parents, his siblings, some colleagues that, to him, were still relative strangers. *Those visits were weird.* He underwent a barrage of assessments—physiological, neurological, biological. He felt like every part of him had been poked and prodded or had blood drawn from it, and when that wasn't happening he had visits from occupational therapists, psychologists, neurologists and the surgical team, who'd given him the low-down on his small procedure.

Most importantly, throughout it all, he had remained *stable* and his observations had been normal. He was ready now. Anxious to leave the hospital walls and get home. Desperate to get back and see if being there would spark anything.

No memories had yet returned, despite Em's frequent visits with accompanying photos and videos of their wedding and the opening of the Monterey. She'd been so keen to show him what they had done. What they had enjoyed. But it had been like looking at photos of a stranger, even though he was in them. It had left him feeling disconcerted. As if he was in a strange bubble.

The waiting to leave hospital was more than

a little infuriating, and over the last few days he'd found himself snapping at various people. The psychology team had reassured him and Emily that this was normal, as he adjusted to his new self and situation, and offered to assess him every month, for as long as he felt the need to talk about it. Mood swings, apparently, were to be expected.

He wasn't sure he did want to talk about it. Not to them, anyway. They'd already cottoned on to the fact that he didn't seem delighted at the idea of becoming a father, and he'd grown to hate his sessions with them, knowing that they would return to the questions he dreaded. He'd even tried sharing his frustration with Emily, but it seemed as if she didn't know anything about Serena.

Was that possible? That they'd been married for eighteen months and he hadn't told her? That had kept him silent on all fronts and contributed to his anger.

So he was particularly pleased that *today* the doctors had finally decided that he could return home—with the understanding that he wasn't to work for a further three months.

'But I can go in and look around? Get familiar with what's going on?' he'd asked.

'Sure. But no working. You won't be covered insurance-wise.'

And with that dire warning they'd left his bedside.

And now Emily was at his side in the car, driving them home.

She seemed really nervous. Edgy. Fidgety. But he put that down to the fact that for the last few weeks the hospital staff had been around to look after him and make sure he was recovering properly. Now that safety barrier would be gone and it would just be down to the two of them.

Well…nearly three of them.

Sam swallowed and tried not to think of the baby. Emily was nearly eleven weeks now, and apparently she was booked in for a scan in a few days. He would have to go with her. Act the dutiful husband and hold her hand if she'd let him—he'd noticed a curious reluctance and hesitation on Emily's part to be physical with him—whilst they squeezed on that cold blue gel and then smile inanely at the images on screen.

He *so wanted* to be happy about this. And a

part of him was. But whenever he thought about them having a baby he pictured his baby sister Serena and what had happened to her when he'd been left in charge…

A car horn sounded, pulling him back to reality, and he flinched, looking across at his wife driving the car.

'Aren't you scared?'

'Of what?'

He wanted to know if she was afraid of becoming a parent. It had to be a big deal for anyone, right? But something stopped him from asking that particular question.

'Driving. After the accident…'

She shook her head, her honey-blonde hair shifting around her shoulders like velvet. 'I was. Not now. But I'm being very careful. We can't just stop doing things because they make us afraid.'

Depends what worries you.

He smiled and glanced out at the streams of traffic. He knew this road. Knew this area. But he had no idea where they were headed except for the fact that Emily was taking them home.

Home. Would he recognise it? Would it spark

a memory? Something—even if it was a little blurry? The doctors at the hospital had told them both that the memories *might* return, and that they might either come all at once or he'd experience the odd one or two at strange moments, in totally unexpected ways.

Brains were mysterious creatures.

Pulling off the freeway, Emily took a slip road and drove for a few more miles through beautiful streets lined with lush green trees and neat sidewalks. He saw a young woman walking a poodle that had been groomed to within an inch of its life, trotting along like a dressage horse. He saw beautiful properties, secure within their walls and at the end of long driveways, as they drove on beneath the heat of the sun in their dark saloon car, and then suddenly they were slowing and turning into a driveway.

He looked up.

A majestic house sat before him. Perfectly white, it glimmered in the midday heat against the glorious blue sky backdrop. It looked *palatial*. Like something fit for a film star or a minor member of royalty.

This is ours?

He tried to picture himself wanting to buy this and could see its perks. It was prestigious, and screamed quality, with tall oak front doors and what seemed like hundreds of windows flashing reflections of the sun into his eyes as they approached up the long, smooth driveway. It was very different from his childhood home.

As they neared, he saw grey clothed *staff* come near the car and open their car doors.

'Welcome back, Mr Saint! So good to see you up and about.'

He smiled at faces he didn't know and stepped out, looking around him. Emily appeared to be much more comfortable with her surroundings than he did, and she quickly indicated to the staff to take their bags from the trunk.

The bags were quickly hurried inside as Sam looked about him at the gardens, which were lush with green leafy trees and all-white flowers and blooms. 'It's beautiful.'

'You picked it. Don't you remember?'

He heard the trepidation in her voice. The hope that he would remember. He hated disappointing her. 'I'm sorry. I don't.'

He needed control of his life back. Something

he hadn't had whilst he'd been stuck in a hospital bed as a passive observer.

'Let's go in. All your things are inside—there might be something...'

Something about the way her voice sounded made him look at her in question. Was it just the amnesia that was making him feel...? *I'm in the dark...*

It was a weird sensation, but the doctors had told him he would feel like this. That he was not to ponder on it, or worry about it, that it was normal. It was probably just him being over-sensitive right now.

Shrugging it off, he took her hand and clasped it tightly, kissing the back of it. Then he smiled at her and nodded. 'Let's do it.'

And they walked inside.

Sam had imagined that this would be *a moment*. A moment when a flood of memories would assail him. He would spot something—a chair, a table, a painting or piece of art, perhaps—that would ignite a memory that had lain dormant and hidden behind *the wall*.

But, looking around him, he felt—and remembered—nothing. He tried not to be too disappointed. But it was hard. He'd told himself in the hospital that when he got home he would remember. That walking through the door into familiar surroundings would give his brain the nudge it needed to start releasing the information he craved.

The fact that his brain was failing him—that his memories were refusing to leap to the surface of his mind—frustrated him. He was a man who had always been perfectly in control of everything, and the fact that he couldn't even force his own brain to do something made him feel angry inside.

Emily let go of his hand and stepped away from him to lay her bag and keys down on a table. 'Anything?'

Gritting his teeth, he shook his head, trying not to be angry with himself. 'No.'

She stared at him for a while. 'Don't worry. Something will trigger it. I'll show you around.'

And she took him from room to room. Sitting room, dining room, library, study, kitchen, utility, staff quarters, the guest bedrooms, the bathrooms, shower rooms, games room… Even all the storage rooms and up into the roof space, which had been converted into yet another guest room. They were all *beautiful.* Elegantly designed. Minimalist. Expensive and sumptuous.

Remembered?

Not at all.

All the belongings, all the possessions that Emily pointed out, convinced he would remember, meant nothing. He *felt* nothing.

A simmering rage bubbled away beneath the surface of his neutral face. And for some reason he felt anger towards Emily. As if it was somehow *her* fault that he couldn't remember. He knew it wasn't. It was just because she was the closest person to him and he so desperately wanted to remember for *her* delight. *Her* joy. Plus, it would also prove to him that he could somehow conquer the two years that had been taken from him. Two years of missed birthdays and celebrations. All of it. He could somehow claim it *back.*

There had to be *something.* Something that would bring back who he was. All that he had lost and then, hopefully, somehow he would have the strength to tackle the next great challenge that awaited them both.

Awaited *him*.

Because how could he be a father when he couldn't even remember creating their child?

'And this…'

Emily swept another door open. Another opportunity for his mind to let him down. He wasn't sure he wanted to look—wasn't sure he wanted to face that part of himself again—but he did, because Emily was being so supportive.

'…is the master bedroom. Our room.'

He stepped in, his gaze instantly drawn to the large king-sized bed in the centre, a mix of blindingly white bedding with gold-accented cushions. There were so many of them! Did they have to throw them all off the bed to get—?

Emily pinned to the bed, gazing up at him, smiling wickedly, her hair spread out in wild abandon across the gold cushions, the tassels weaving into her hair, making it seem as if she had strands of pure gold in it. His lips trailing down her neck, feather-light, her laughter, her—

The sudden onslaught of memory caused Sam to reach out a hand to steady himself.

'Sam—you okay?' She caught up to him and laid a hand upon his arm, her face full of concern.

'Yeah, I'm fine, I—'

A gold cushion being thrown at his chest from across the room. Emily growling with irritation, stalking away from him, yanking the bedroom door open so hard it left a small dent in the wall. 'I hate you!'

Sam blinked and looked behind him. At the wall. There was a small dent.

'Sam? Have you remembered something?'

He met her gaze. 'You were angry with me.'

She blanched. 'What?'

'In this room—you threw a cushion at me… one of those off the bed. I was over here.' He stepped over to the part of the room that he'd seen in his memory. 'You threw it and you stormed out of the door and yelled from the corridor that you hated me.'

Emily looked awkwardly at the floor and he could see that she was biting her lip.

What had happened to make her say she *hated* him? She hadn't said he annoyed her, or irritated her, she hadn't said, *I really don't like you sometimes, Sam*. She'd said 'hate'.

What had they been arguing about? Had he

done something wrong? Had she? 'What was that about?'

She grimaced. 'I'm not sure.'

He pictured the look on her face as she'd stormed away. 'You seemed pretty serious.'

Emily swallowed and sat down on the edge of the bed, fidgeting nervously. She patted the bedspread beside her and he sat down, waiting for her explanation.

'Things have been…tense sometimes.'

'Sometimes?'

'A lot.'

She seemed embarrassed to say it. As if she was letting him down by telling him this. But even though it was hurtful to hear he'd rather have the truth.

'What about?'

She sighed and her shoulders sagged. 'Family stuff. We had got to a point where we were hardly talking. When we did, we argued. Over and over again.'

'We were that bad?' He hated to ask, but Emily wasn't making it sound as if things had been good between them.

'We crashed the car arguing.'

He stared hard at the floor. 'God, Em, I'm really sorry.'

He felt the distance between them then. Even though they were next to each other on the bed she wasn't leaning into him for comfort—she wasn't seeking his support. She was stiff and straight beside him, eyes downcast.

How had things got so bad between them, so quickly? Was this why she looked startled each time he tried to hold her hand or kiss her?

'At least you remembered something…' she muttered.

He stared at the pristine white carpet on the floor. 'Yeah. I guess I did.'

Emily led Sam into his private office, hoping that *this room* above all others would mean something to her husband.

This was such a weird situation for them both. *She knew this man.* And yet because he couldn't remember the last two years it felt to her, in a way, that she was leading a stranger around their house. Seeing the way he looked at things in wonder and surprise, seeing things familiar to her but brand-new to him.

Hadn't he stood in this very doorway and kissed her? Hadn't he sat at this desk for many hours, talking on the phone, arranging galas and press nights for the Monterey? Hadn't they had one of their worst arguments in here? Leading to the first time Sam had stormed from the house, tearing down the driveway in the car so hard he'd left tyre marks?

He'd had a memory come back. A bad one. It was a scary sign. *Good* that he was remembering, but *bad* because of what it might mean for their relationship now.

It was clear that their problems weren't just going to disappear, the way his memories had. Whether he remembered their issues or not, Sam was still the same man and she needed to remember that. The issue here wasn't just the amnesia. They still had the problems of their marriage to solve, and if they were going to do that then they would have to start communicating and working together. Something they hadn't done for a long time.

She watched as he entered, noting the way his fingers trailed over the large glass-topped desk, the way he picked up the Murano glass paperweight that they'd bought in Paris, the way he stared hard at the picture of himself and Emily standing in front of the Monterey on the day of its Grand Opening. Their smiling faces, the green-garbed staff standing behind them, all with their hands in the air cheering.

She *wanted* him to remember it all. She really did. How else were they both going to recover? Right now Sam seemed happy about the pregnancy, and he was clearly wanting to be physical with her. Kissing her. Reaching out for her hand. Giving her the love that she'd craved. The *closeness* and *intimacy* that had been sadly lacking in their relationship since the arguments had started. But it was still difficult for her. Strange…

Because she *did* remember.

What would happen tonight? Would he sleep in their bed? Lately he'd been sleeping at work, and when he *had* made it home he'd either told her he'd sleep on the couch or go to a guest room. That had been embarrassing—the staff certainly knew—and also deeply hurtful.

Was it wrong to wish desperately that Sam wouldn't recall that part of their relationship?

Was it wrong to be putting all her hope into this second chance they'd been given? Was it wrong to wish that Sam wouldn't regain his memories at all?

Of course it is! And I feel terrible for even giving those thoughts space in my head!

It was as if Sam were two different people right now, though she knew that it wasn't really true.

He's the same man and I need to remember that. The man who wouldn't talk to me is the same man standing next to me right now. And I'm not sure I know how we're going to sort this.

There was a baby that would need its father. Emily hadn't had one of those. Or a mother. Not really. She had been passed to an aunt by her mother so she could go rushing off after some ageing rock star and travel with him to gigs, and after that last time she'd just never come back. Even now Emily had no idea where or who she really was. Her mother had a name, but she didn't know more than that.

Staying with her Aunt Sylvia hadn't provided much insight either. Sylvia had not been a big fan of her sister, and had resented being left with a young toddler who made lots of noise and even more mess. Emily had soon stopped asking Sylvia and her Uncle Martin questions they never had answers to.

Who's my real mummy?

When is she coming back?

Does she love me?

The sound of drawers being opened and closed brought Emily back to the present. If Sam, now sitting behind his desk, was looking for something personal there he'd be disappointed. They only contained work-related paperwork and files. He looked lost in a world that should have been oh-so-familiar to him.

'It'll come back, Sam. Maybe not today. But it will.' She hated to see him hurting. It hurt her in return.

He smiled at her attempt to comfort him, but it was bitter. 'Well, a bit did come back today—only it wasn't what I expected.'

He shook his head, as if he couldn't quite believe all that she had told him. The bad memory had clearly rocked him to his core and he seemed to be thrown by that. He'd believed them to be happy. Why wouldn't they be? She wished she could explain it to him, but she didn't have any answers herself.

'We have to believe that things will get better.'

'Speaks the eternal optimist.'

Pulling deep within herself, she leaned over his desk and made him look her in the eyes. 'You're a fighter, Sam. We would never have got the Monterey started if it hadn't been for your vision. You've got to believe that all those memories in there...the ones that make you *you*... they're still in there. They're not lost. Not really. You just don't have access yet.'

'Like membership to an exclusive club?'

She nodded. 'Exactly.'

'I'm not sure I want membership to the bad marriage club.'

Emily stood up straight. 'Me neither. But we're in it, and we both have to work together if we want to make changes.'

He looked about the room one more time, before he stood and tucked his chair under his desk. 'You're right. We do.'

The telephone call came as they were heading downstairs. Emily's cell vibrated in her pocket and she knew immediately what the call was about the second she saw the name of the caller.

'Em? It's Marc—Sophie's husband. Her waters have broken and she's having strong contractions. We're coming in to the Monterey.'

Marc and Sophie were a couple who had come to the Monterey for fertility treatment and had conceived their much wanted first child through IVF. Sophie was terrified of both hospitals and needles—something she'd had to overcome to get through her hormone treatments and appointments. Emily had *promised* from the very beginning that she would be there to help them deliver their child, and Sophie had come to rely on Emily being there as her safe harbour, her port in a storm.

Emily's heart was torn between Sophie's labour and staying with Sam, whom she'd just brought home.

'Hi, Marc. I'm at home at the moment…hang on—' She held the phone to her chest so she could privately talk to Sam. 'It's clients. Sophie and Marc? The IVF couple? Sophie's in labour—I promised I would be there.'

Sam looked blank at the names, but he nodded anyway. He knew that work was important to them both. 'You should go.'

'You've only just come home. You need someone with you.'

He smiled. 'I have *staff*, remember? Go be with Sophie.'

She loved it that this part of Sam was still here. The need to be there for their patients, putting them first, staying true to the promises they made to care for their charges.

Em lifted the phone back to her ear. 'I'll come in. How far away are you?'

'I'm already driving, but traffic is heavy. Twenty minutes?'

'I'll meet you at the entrance. See you soon.' She ended the call and smiled at Sam. 'Thank you.'

'Hey, it's not a problem. It's what we do. Go on. You don't want to miss it.'

No. She didn't. She laid a hand on his arm, smiling, and then started running down the stairs, grabbing her purse and keys from the table and hurrying out of the front door.

She hated leaving him alone. But perhaps he needed some time in their home to wander about and look at things without feeling under pressure to remember.

She told herself it was a good thing she was heading in to the Monterey. She was about to see the outcome of a long, difficult journey for Sophie and Marc. This was what their work was all about. Welcoming new life into the world. Celebrating that.

And soon it would be her and Sam's turn.

One day. Maybe.

Sophie was labouring *hard*. Her normally calm and serene face was now red and creased, and her eyes were closed tight as she tried to breathe through a contraction.

Her husband Marc stood by her, one hand clutching hers, the other rubbing hard at the small of his wife's back.

Sophie had not wanted to get into bed. She'd said it had made her too uncomfortable. She wanted to get into the large birthing tub, which was currently filling with water.

'How much longer?' Sophie asked, blowing away the last of the contraction.

Emily checked the temperature of the water,

which was perfect. 'Okay. You can get into the pool now.'

Marc helped his wife strip off the last of her garments and held her arm as she gingerly stepped over the side of the pool and lowered herself, settling into the warm embrace of the water.

'Oh, my God, this is bliss!'

Marc laughed. 'That's not what you said a moment ago.'

Emily smiled at them both. It was a surprise to a lot of husbands that their partners often felt so much better between contractions. Making a note in Sophie's file, she entered the time her patient had got into the pool and then got a Sonicaid device and listened to the baby's heartbeat by pressing the probe against Sophie's abdomen. There was a little sound of interference, and then a strong, steady heartbeat sounded out in the small room.

'Sounds perfect, Sophie. You're on track. Any urge to push?'

Her patient wiped her brow. 'I'm not sure. I think so…a little with that last one.'

'Okay, let's see how you are with the next few

contractions and if that feeling increases we'll check to see if you're fully dilated.'

Sophie nodded, and then braced herself against the pool as another contraction hit.

Emily watched as Marc helped his wife through it, surreptitiously timing the contraction. It was good and strong. At least a minute in length, which was what they needed. Sophie had to be close, and Emily felt a ball of excitement in the pit of her stomach, as she always did when a birth was near.

This was what she lived for. Bringing new life into the world. It was something that had fascinated her ever since she'd seen a documentary on the television one evening as a child. Sylvia and Martin had gone out to an event at their local church and Emily had turned on the television out of boredom.

She'd hardly ever seen the television switched on. Sylvia and Martin had preferred to read, or listen to a play on the radio. But Emily had known it was a source of endless fascination for her schoolfriends and so she'd switched it on that night and found a documentary about a maternity unit. There, on screen, she had watched and learned about the way babies came into the world, and she'd been captured by its raw beauty, its power. She'd been surprised to discover tears trickling down her cheeks when she'd witnessed how overwhelmed the parents were by their new child.

I want to do that.

Seeing love, in all its raw glory, was something that she'd craved.

Did my mom act like that with me?

From that day forward she'd dreamt of finding a man who would look into her eyes like that, with so much love and pride. Of carrying her own baby and experiencing that rush of love and joy as she pushed her baby into the world. Never to be alone again…never to be forgotten. Never again to be that lonely little girl, sitting in her room, wondering where her mother was.

'Emily? I need to push.'

'Okay, just breathe through it this time. I need to check you first.'

Marc glanced nervously at her. 'Shouldn't she just push?'

'If she's not fully dilated yet it could cause

swelling around the cervix and make her delivery difficult.'

Marc looked confused, but nodded, because he trusted her implicitly.

With the contraction over, Emily put on some gloves and checked Sophie. She smiled. 'You're ten centimetres! You're all set.'

Sophie started to cry. 'Oh, my God! It's happening—it's really happening! Marc?' She turned to her husband and clutched his hand as if she would never let go. 'We're going to have our baby soon.'

Marc kissed his wife. 'I know, honey. I'm so proud of you.'

Sophie laid her forehead against her husband's and then started grimacing as the next contraction hit. 'What do I do, Emily?'

'I want you to take a deep breath and then bear down into your bottom until I say stop, okay?'

Sophie bore down, the strain showing in the redness of her face.

'Seven, eight, nine, ten. Okay, another breath and push again!'

Emily counted the seconds away. Sophie and Marc were so close now to seeing their miracle baby. They'd tried so hard to get pregnant, and for a long time had thought that it wouldn't happen for them. Sophie and Marc hadn't met until they were in their early forties, and after a year of trying had come to the Monterey in desperation, afraid that time was running out for both of them.

Two cycles of IVF had failed, but on their third try they'd been successful. Sophie had been a model patient—eating right, exercising, looking after herself—and Emily knew this baby was going to be cherished.

'Oh, my God, Em, how much longer?' Sophie groaned.

'Not long! I can see a head of thick dark hair! Do you want to touch?'

'Really?' Sophie reached down and felt the top of her baby's head. 'Oh!'

Emily smiled and shone a light so Marc could see, too. 'What do you think, Dad? Takes after you?'

Marc blinked away tears. 'This is…' He couldn't speak any more. He just clutched his wife's hand and kissed the back of it. 'Come on, Soph, you can do it—you're nearly there.'

It took just four more pushes and the head crowned, emerged and restituted, so that the baby faced Sophie's inner right thigh.

'Head's out, Sophie! Just one more push and you'll be a mum!'

Sophie bore down as the next contraction came.

Emily supported the baby's head and body as it came out, and looked up at Sophie. 'Are you ready to take your baby?'

Sophie looked down, gasped aloud, and then reached for her newborn. 'Oh, my God!' She pulled the baby upward and rested it against her belly, and then burst into tears as her baby let out its first beautiful cry.

'You did it, Soph! You did it!' Marc laid his hand on his newborn child and began to cry.

The dads' crying always got to Emily. She had to bite her lip to stop *herself* from crying. She didn't know what it was, but she'd seen this so many times and it never got old. It was a privilege, and one that she cherished.

'Congratulations.' She clamped the cord and handed the scissors to Marc. "Cut between the clamps.'

He did so, and laughed, laying his head against his wife's.

'Did you see what flavour you got?'

Sophie and Marc had wanted it to be a surprise.

Sophie sniffed and wiped at her eyes, before she looked down and lifted up one of her baby's legs. 'It's a girl! Marc, we have a daughter!'

Marc kissed her and put his arm around his wife.

Emily laid a towel over the baby. It soon got wet, but it helped to keep the baby warm. Sophie wanted a natural stage three, allowing the placenta to come out on its own, without the aid of drugs, and once that was done and had been checked, Emily helped Sophie get out of the bath and onto the bed.

She wrapped fresh towels around their daughter and checked Sophie for tears. All looked well. She'd done brilliantly.

'You haven't torn, Sophie. That's brilliant.'

She stared for a moment at the family picture of Sophie, Marc and their new daughter on the bed. A solid family unit.

She wanted that for her and Sam. That dream

image that she'd built up in her imagination since she had first seen it on television. A mum. A dad. A baby. All wrapped together in the strong bonds of love. United.

There *had* to be a way for them to get there.

'Have you got a name for her yet?'

Marc looked up and smiled. 'Xanthe.'

Emily nodded. 'That's beautiful.'

She let the family have a few moments together, and then took Xanthe to check her over. All looked well, and she scored high on the APGAR, so she bundled Xanthe up again and handed her back to her parents. No doubt this little girl would be treasured and loved for her lifetime.

'I'll leave you guys alone for a moment. Give me a buzz if you need anything.'

Emily slipped from the room and went to write up her notes about the delivery. It was wonderful when deliveries went as smoothly as this one, and Sophie and Marc—who had been through the mill—deserved their happy-ever-after.

In her office, Emily was lost in thoughts about what would happen in the future for her and Sam. Would he regain his memories and know the whole truth about their marriage? Really, she *did* want him to, because then they could work through their issues. She just wanted them to have some time first. Time to reconnect, to fall back in love, time to strengthen their relationship.

Was that so bad? Wanting the best for them? Wanting their relationship to succeed? This time could give them what they'd never had before. The opportunity to open up to each other and work out whatever the real problem was. Because there had to be a reason Sam hadn't wanted to talk to her before.

Now, because of the accident, because of what had happened, Sam was still reeling, and he needed to anchor himself. Find himself. And if she could help him to do that then maybe, just maybe, he would see just how much she was fighting for their marriage. How much she wanted them to succeed. Surely he did, too, otherwise he wouldn't be so upset that it had gone wrong?

He'd loved her once—she just wanted to reinforce those feelings somehow. So that if everything went pear-shaped after his memories returned they would have a much better chance of staying together and having the perfect family that she wanted for them.

Her gaze fell upon the one picture she allowed herself in her office. It was of her and Sam, in front of the Eiffel Tower in Paris during their honeymoon. They'd had such a brilliant time there. It was an enchanting city, and the way she'd felt for Sam there had been overwhelming.

It was a pity they weren't there now.

But what if we could be?

The doctors had said that the best way to help Sam find his memories would be to immerse him in experience—the sights, sounds, smells of something familiar. What if they went back to Paris? Sam was signed off work for a few months. If they could get a Fit to Fly certificate from his consultant they could go back there and experience that magical place once again!

A spark of hope ignited in her chest and she stared at the photo once more. And if Sam's memories *did* come back by then it would be too late, because he would have fallen in love with her all over again!

They *needed* this.

In the past two years Sam had been working hard to get the Monterey up and running, working tirelessly behind the scenes. She'd barely seen him, and they'd argued when she had. This would be good for *her*—not just Sam.

Emily smiled and turned to her computer. Accessing the internet, she found a local travel agent and picked up the phone and dialled their number.

There was no harm in finding out.

CHAPTER FOUR

AIR FRANCE FLEW out of Los Angeles International, and after eleven hours and fifty minutes Emily and Sam touched down at Charles de Gaulle Airport, north-east of Paris.

Emily's excitement levels were high. Paris held such great memories for her and their relationship. When they'd come here before they'd been honeymooning, newly married, accomplished owners of a successful new birth centre business and blissfully happy. Everything had been going so well for them.

After making the decision to return to Paris, Emily had returned home from her successful delivery of Marc and Sophie's baby and blurted out her idea.

'Sam? We should go to Paris!'

'What?'

'We should go back to Paris. Where we honeymooned. Remember the doc said that we should immerse you in sights and sounds and aromas. Can you think of a better place than one where we were so happy?'

'I don't remember Paris.'

'Exactly! If your memory doesn't return there...well, we'll just make new memories. That both of us will remember this time.'

Sam had laughed at her enthusiasm, but then he'd seen how determined she was. He'd called his consultant to check that it was okay for him to fly. His doctor had said that he didn't think it was a problem. Sam wasn't on oxygen, he didn't have any open wounds from surgery, and air travel was only usually restricted for seven to ten days post-neurosurgery. Sam had been recovering for a month now.

A Fit to Fly certificate had been arranged and before Sam had known what was happening they'd been booked onto a flight the next day.

Emily had meant it. The last time they'd visited she had truly fallen in love with the city, and had hated having to leave after their ten days there. As they'd risen into the sky on their way home Emily had looked out of the window at the city dropping away beneath her and whispered, *'I'll come back.'*

And here they were. Strolling through the airport, through the domed concourses, dragging their bags behind them, revelling in the hustle and bustle as hundreds of different voices and languages could be heard around them.

Despite looking in a shop window and gaping at a beautiful dress that she would normally have stopped to buy, she was so keen to get them to their hotel that she quickly hurried along.

Outside they found a *station de taxi* waiting to pick up passengers. They hailed one and got inside.

'Bonjour, monsieur...madame. Où?'

Emily smiled. 'Shangri-La Hotel, *s'il vous plaît.*' She turned to her husband and smiled.

'Shangri-La? Sounds...exotic.'

'It was where we had our honeymoon—*and* I managed to get us the exact same suite we stayed in the last time.'

Sam nodded in appreciation. 'You *have* been busy.'

'I'd do anything to get you back, Sam.' She

felt her cheeks flush. 'I mean…to get your memory back.'

He smiled at her. He knew what she meant. Their relationship had clearly been faltering. From that one memory it looked as if it had become a war zone. It pained him to think how bad it had got for them and, like Em, he too wanted this trip to work.

And if you wanted to get the romance back, the love, where else to go but the most romantic city in the world?

'Thanks, Em. You've been great through all of this. The accident, looking after me… It can't have been easy.'

She appreciated his acknowledgement of all her hard work. 'Well, morning sickness didn't help.'

She looked out of the window as her eye caught a glimpse of some hares or rabbits darting across the grass beside the road, so she didn't notice his gaze darken at her reminder of the pregnancy.

If she were honest, she'd admit that he'd been distant from her the last couple of days. They'd still not yet made love since his return from hospital, which didn't surprise her. Not after she'd told him how much they'd been arguing. Perhaps he had felt he couldn't approach her?

But she'd not pushed for it either. She hadn't slept with her husband for a couple of months, and it would have been strange for them to have tried, knowing how bad their marriage had become.

Sam had cited headaches, which she knew were to be expected, and she'd been grateful. She needed time herself to work up to the idea of becoming intimate with her husband once again.

It hadn't taken Sam long to return to his study in their house, determined to bring himself up to speed with what had happened in the last two years. Sometimes—just as before the accident—he'd fallen asleep there. It had removed the pressure and she'd been thankful for that.

Before, there'd always been a reason why he couldn't talk, or why he couldn't come home. It had made her uneasy, and she didn't want to return to the pattern they had fallen into. So arranging this trip together had been good. They were united in the idea of working to get each other back.

Emily *needed* to get Sam back. The good Sam.

The Sam who loved her and adored her. The Sam who was happy about the baby and had beamed a smile whenever he'd seen her arrive at the hospital. The husband who wanted to hold her hand. Be near her. Touch her.

She missed his touch.

It wasn't just sex with Sam—it never had been. He had always made love to her, making her feel cherished and adored. As if he worshipped her. As if he couldn't get enough of her. The way she felt…the way she tasted. And afterwards, when they'd lain in each other's arms, sated and complete, warm and loved, she'd never wished for anything more.

To lose that—to lose that precious physical connection that they'd once shared—had almost torn her apart.

As she gazed out of the taxi window, her fingers fiddling with the pendant around her neck, she hoped fervently that back here, in this place, they would be able to reclaim that part of their marriage. Not just the sex, the making love, but the closeness she'd once had with him.

They'd had it good once. They could have it again.

* * *

The drive to the hotel took about forty-five minutes. Emily felt so happy to be in Paris and she clutched Sam's hand, squeezing his fingers every time she turned to look at him and smile. She gazed at the tree-lined roads, the relaxed unhurried pedestrians and the tourists ambling along the sidewalks, gasping when there was a break in the treeline or buildings and she caught a sweeping view of the city.

This feels like home to me.

She gazed at the varied architecture, from modern glass and steel to the more aged and authentic French buildings built during the reign of Louis XIV. There was such an eclectic mix here, and it never failed to astound her.

Sam, on the other hand, was looking at the city with new eyes. She watched him to see if anything seemed familiar—a sight, a sound. But he gazed at the city as if he had never seen it before and she felt her shoulders slump.

It's still early, though. We haven't got to our suite yet. Surely he must remember that?

It would be good if some of the memories, when they returned, were *good* ones! She hated to think that all he would remember would be the bad.

Arriving outside the hotel, they paid their driver and stepped out.

The Shangri-La was beautiful to look at. Positioned in the sixteenth *arrondissement*, it was a nineteenth-century decadent-looking structure, apparently originally the private mansion of Prince Roland Bonaparte, the nephew of Napoleon. Once named the Palais Iéna, it stood in a tasteful corner of Paris, resting within the shadow of the elegant Eiffel Tower.

Sam looked up at the hotel and felt a sense of awe. History, *seeped* from this place. The entranceway with its sturdy white columns, and above the mass of ornate curlicued iron balconies, made him feel a tiny bit insignificant against this backdrop of important French history.

A uniformed porter assisted them with their bags into the hotel reception area and they stepped into a world of elegance. Even the floor was beautiful, and in the centre was a gold and glass table set with a generous, fragrant bouquet of lilies.

Sam stood back as Emily took care of all the arrangements and glanced around as he waited, studying the features, trying to see if anything would trigger a memory.

Nothing.

Maybe he needed a little more time? Perhaps if he relaxed a bit more then the memories might return? He'd had a couple. Back home. Fleeting ones, but still…it was better than nothing.

He was glad that he had agreed to this trip. Emily had seemed so sure that it was the right thing for them to do, and Sam had felt the same way after a moment or two of thought. It was what they needed—he wanted to get their marriage back on track as much as she did.

After learning that he'd lost two years of his life, and discovering that his business had become such a success, he'd felt keen to catch up on what was happening at the Monterey. But once he'd had that flashback…well, it hadn't taken him but a moment to agree to come here.

It was why he had closeted himself in his office, despite his physical need to reconnect with Em. Catching up on paperwork, accounts, reports, assessments, staff training was the only way he knew to allow her space. He understood her distance, her reticence to kiss him, to touch him.

The birth centre had been his dream and the fact that he'd missed its launch galled him. His wedding. His honeymoon. It was all gone—hidden behind *that wall.*

He'd noticed the little looks she'd given him when she had found him in his office yet again. The looks she'd tried to hide when he had not returned to their marital bed. Had they been looks of relief or upset?

He wanted to. Of course he did. He loved her. But… Sam was a driven man, and work was important to him. Now more than ever. Emily was carrying his child, and his sense of responsibility to take care of them both lay heavy upon his shoulders. But beneath that something didn't feel right. Knowing that they'd argued, that he'd upset her… The *timing* didn't feel right. It was awkward, and because he didn't do well with *awkward* he'd focused on the one part of his life where he did do well. Work.

His thoughts drifted back to the scan. He should be pleased it had gone so well. The baby had looked good, there had been no concerns over the measurement of the nuchal fold at the back of the baby's neck, growth looked consistent with dates. The pregnancy was going well.

He should have felt joy.

But all he had been able to feel was fear.

What if he couldn't protect their baby? What if he failed their child? What if the same thing happened as before? Serena had been in *his care* and she had died. How could he possibly get things right for this baby?

Had he been mad, thinking that coming to Paris was a good idea? Their relationship was not the joyful coupling he'd thought it was back when he'd proposed. They had been married for just over a year and already they were in trouble. But why?

Emily had mentioned his not wanting a baby, so she knew that much about his feelings. Obviously the married Sam had felt it easier to say than today's Sam. But it was becoming increasingly obvious that she knew nothing about *why* he didn't want a child. And that bothered him. He'd always assumed he would tell her at some point. Why hadn't he? Because of all their arguments?

Because you're afraid to admit what you did.

What would she think of him? An OB/GYN who delivered countless babies, head of a fabulous five-star birth centre, who had failed to realise that his baby sister had died?

The sound of the lift arriving brought Sam back to the present, and he and Emily followed the porter out of the lift and down the corridor to their suite.

'What do you think, Sam?' Emily asked as the porter swept open the door to their room.

It was tremendously beautiful. Painted in a soft cream, with original features and gold-draped windows, the room was littered with period furniture. Light from the sliding French doors that opened out onto a broad balcony welcomed them in, and just off to the right, almost within touching distance, was the tower that everyone recognised and thought of when they went to Paris.

'It's amazing.'

'It's our original suite. The one we honeymooned in.'

He turned to face her, hearing the nerves in her voice.

The honeymoon suite. A room built for seduction and intimacy. Was she nervous of being with him? Of beginning that side of their relationship again?

Sam tried to give her a reassuring smile. He couldn't blame her. She was doing so much to help him find his memories again. She was doing what she thought was right and he couldn't, *shouldn't* complain. But he was feeling the weight of her expectations and felt terrible at letting her down, because nothing about the room was sparking anything for him. And he was feeling terribly guilty about the state of their marriage. This trip *had* to work! He wanted her back. He wanted them *happy*.

Emily tipped the porter and he disappeared without notice. Then she joined her husband out on the balcony as they gazed out over the city. 'Can you feel it, Sam?'

'Feel what?'

'The city, welcoming us back.'

He smiled and reached out to curl his fingers around her own. He just wanted to touch her for a moment. To acknowledge why they were here. But he wouldn't put any pressure on her until she was ready.

'Let's go out and explore. What should we do first, do you think?'

'Well, I don't know about you, but me and the baby are starving. Can we go get something to eat? Find a little café or restaurant?'

Her reminder about the baby pierced his conscience, but he pasted a smile over his face. He couldn't let her know how concerned he was. What would she think of him if he told her the truth? That he didn't feel able to protect the baby? At least whilst it still lay within her womb it was safe, and he had no concerns about her delivering. Both of them were trained for that. It was *afterwards* that worried him. He wouldn't be looking after the baby for one night, the way he'd had to babysit Serena. This baby—their baby—he'd be looking after for the *rest of his life*.

'Food sounds good. Let's go.'

They walked through the streets hand in hand, soaking up the sights, sounds and smells of Paris.

Walking past a bakery made Emily salivate with anticipation, but walking past a *poissonnerie*—a fishmongers—made her feel a little queasy.

'Maybe you should stay away from seafood, Em,' Sam joked as he wrapped a reassuring arm around her shoulders and led her towards the River Seine.

They headed down to the Jardins du Trocadero, admiring the fountain and the views of the river, before heading deep into the city, wandering down small cobbled streets, looking for something small and chic and different. Eventually they found exactly what they were looking for.

Gino's Cottage was a rooftop restaurant. All the diners got to sit out on the terrace at long banqueting tables, with views towards the Palais de Chaillot in the distance.

They were soon seated, and they ordered themselves something to drink—wine for Sam and sparkling water for Emily—before they perused the menu.

'It feels so good to be back here.'

Sam looked at her over his menu. 'We came here before?'

'No, not this place. I meant Paris. I loved it here when we came for our honeymoon.'

'Can you tell me about it? Some of the things we did?'

She blushed a little. 'Well, not all of them. Certainly not in public!'

He smiled.

'I think I'm going to have the *bruschetta des tomates* to start. What do you fancy?'

'Hmm…' His eyes scanned the options. 'I think I'll join you with that. What about your main course?'

'Hmm…lasagne, I think, for me.'

'And I'll have the carbonara.'

She laughed. 'Can you believe we've come to France and ended up choosing Italian food?'

'We'll go full-on French tomorrow.'

They placed their order with the waiter and Sam took a sip of his wine. It was perfect. Fruity. Crisp. With just a tart enough kick on the back of his throat.

'So, tell me about our first visit.'

Emily's eyes became dreamy, which he had to smile at, and as he stared at his beautiful wife he couldn't help but think just how lucky he was.

'Well, we didn't come out of our room the first day we arrived. We took full advantage of Room Service after we'd...worked up an appetite.'

He noticed her blushes and smiled slightly as his own imagination supplied him with the possibilities of what that might have been like.

She straightened her serviette on her lap. 'We did lots of walking, exploring, trying to find the *real* Paris—you know, stuff off the beaten track. We didn't just want to do the traditional touristy stuff.'

He nodded. 'Tell me one of your favourite places.'

Emily sighed happily in recollection. 'We went to the Bois de Vincennes and rowed out across the lake to the temple on the island. There's a grotto underneath and we went there quite late, at sunset. It was the most beautiful thing I ever saw.'

'We should go again, then.'

'I'd like that.' She smiled at him, and then they said nothing for a while.

Sam gazed at her from across the table and it felt good to have his full attention.

'We have been happy, Sam. I know I said we'd argued, but…there were good times, too.'

'When did it all start to change?'

She shrugged, the shift in her demeanour clear. 'I don't know. It was gradual. I can remember sitting down to dinner with you one night, like we are now, across the table from one another, and I was excited because I was going to suggest we start a family. It meant so much to me, and I honestly believed that it would to you, too. Considering what we both do for a living, it seemed the next natural step. We were married, our business was getting off the ground, financially we were solid. I couldn't see why there would be any objection. I thought that when I suggested having a baby you'd think about it briefly. Mull it over as you sipped your wine and then we'd discuss when we'd start trying.'

'But it didn't go that way?'

Her gaze was downcast, her eyes darkening. 'No. You…you became a different man. The second I mentioned it a wall seemed to come down in front of you. You closed yourself off, told me it wasn't a good idea, and suddenly said you had work to do in your office. You got up and left. That's how it was with us. We never got to talk about the important stuff like that. Work—fine. Business? No problem. Personal stuff? You backed away.'

Sam looked down at the table.

'I left the subject alone for a bit. Things returned to normal. We worked hard. You were doing a lot of fundraising, a lot of galas, a lot of promotion. I started feeling lonely. As if I didn't have a husband any more. That the one I had was married to the Monterey. I tried to ask for a bit more of your time. I wanted to get you alone, so we could talk. But there was only one subject I wanted to talk about and you just kept getting angry so I stopped asking.' She sipped her water. 'We stopped talking to one another entirely—except about business.'

Sam let out a heavy sigh and rubbed at his forehead. 'It was bad, then?'

'It wasn't great.'

The waiter arrived with their starters.

The aroma of their food was delightful, the freshness and richness of the juicy tomatoes could not be questioned, and the bread had definitely been made by hand on site and flavoured with herbs and pepper.

Sam hadn't been sure he wanted to eat after hearing all that, but the sight of the food set his mouth watering.

They ate in silence, and it probably would have continued that way, but he reminded himself that they were here to *solve* their problems.

Sam sought for a brighter topic, so they could start talking again. 'Tell me about our wedding.'

Instantly she smiled warmly at the memories. 'It was a wonderful day. The weather was perfect. Everything went so well. Though I can remember standing outside, waiting to go in, and a honeybee flew under my veil. I panicked so much I think I might have screamed! But thankfully my bridesmaids were much braver than I was and they managed to brush it off me. It set my nerves jangling, but then…when the music started and I walked down the aisle towards you…all my nerves just disappeared. I knew that what I was doing was right, and that the man waiting for me—*you*—was going to make me the happiest woman in the world.'

He smiled and raised his glass to hers, clinking them together.

'We had a huge reception—hundreds came, mostly people *you* knew. We released a pair of doves from the balcony of the hotel, and we had all these cameras on the guests' tables and they each took pictures of what was special for them. I've got all the albums in the house somewhere. I can dig them out for you, if you like?'

He nodded. 'Tell me about the Monterey.'

'What can I say? It's doing better than either of us ever imagined. It helped, I think, that one of our first guests was a Saudi princess who gave birth to twins. She arrived with all these security guards, and she had so many staff, but we were able to accommodate them by allotting them the entire third floor. After that our success rates went through the roof. Everyone wanted to come to us. Everyone wanted to have their babies in the same place that princesses had been born.'

'And the fertility clinic?'

'I'm not sure of the exact numbers, but I believe so far we've helped over a hundred couples to conceive and successfully carry their children to term. Our manager, Edward, would be able to give you exact numbers. Didn't you call him before we left?'

'Yes, I wanted numbers and cost forecasting for the next year.'

Em nodded, aware that Sam had become work-focused yet again, despite all she'd said about the state of their marriage. It was something she was familiar with.

She finished her bruschetta, sliding her knife and fork together on her plate. 'How do you think it's all looking? I try my best to keep myself informed, but the money side of things is not my forte. I prefer the hands-on work.'

'It looks like we're exceeding expectations. I'm happy about that.'

'But…?' She looked at him with concern, knowing there was something else.

'But I'm not happy that our marriage has gone downhill.'

'We were both at fault. We allowed the Monterey to be our main focus, and sadly we forgot to put just as much work into us as we did that.'

'I should never have allowed it to happen.'

'Like I said, it was both of us.'

He appreciated her trying to let him off the hook, but he still felt that it was his fault. 'I still can't believe I don't remember it.'

'You were definitely there.' She gave a slight smile.

'But I don't remember, Em! I want to recall the experience of the rush of the Monterey's opening. The worry about whether we'd succeed and the watching and the observing as everything began to get better. The tweaking of the things that weren't quite right, answering our patients' needs and serving them, making their experience the best they could ever imagine. I don't feel I was part of any of that. I've just been handed dry forecasts and accounts of where we are now and apparently, according to you, work is just fine—but *we* aren't.'

She reached for her glass of water. Sipped it. 'We can be okay again, Sam. That's why we're here. And you *did* experience it. You worked so hard. The memory is in there—you've just got to be patient.'

'I know. It's just…'

'Frustrating?'

He nodded and sat back as their waiter arrived

to clear their dishes. Once he'd disappeared, Sam sat forward again. 'I feel out of place, Em. I know the Monterey is ours, that we made it happen, but I don't *feel* like it's mine. I feel like it's something you've done. That it's been your project and you've just shown it to me. Does that make any sense?'

'A little, yes. But you have to know that it will all come back—you've already experienced one old memory. And when it does…'

He saw a shadow cross her face and knew why she looked so worried. 'Yes?'

'When it does, you'll know…everything.' She forced a smile.

'I hope so. I really do.'

'Me too.' She dabbed at her mouth with the serviette. 'I must just use the ladies' room. Excuse me.'

He watched her hurry away.

He knew why he was really so frustrated at not being there for the Monterey. It had always been *his* big project. *His* dream. He'd put so much work into it when really he should have been putting all the work into his marriage. He could vocalise his concerns about missing out on the Monterey. But he couldn't vocalise about what had gone wrong in his marriage—because Emily didn't yet know about Serena.

I've got to tell her. We won't survive otherwise.

Whilst he waited, he stared out across the darkening evening of Paris. The fairy lights had come on around the terrace, bathing them all in soft white light, but the brightest beacon of all was the lit Eiffel Tower, behind him in the distance.

It was a stunning sight—one they would no doubt be able to enjoy from their hotel window.

Sam hoped Paris would be everything they had planned it to be.

He needed his memories back.

He needed to be the man Emily had fallen in love with.

He needed to be strong.

Needed to know who he was and what he had gone through.

Why couldn't the accident have erased the memory of what happened to Serena?

Dinner was superb. The lasagne that Emily had ordered was deliciously sumptuous, and the chocolate mousse they shared for pudding was soft, rich and velvety.

As they sat drinking coffee Sam asked her an awkward question.

'Considering how things were between us, I take it the baby was a surprise?'

Hurrying to swallow her mouthful of coffee, she almost choked on it. 'Yes. It was a surprise. I didn't even know I was pregnant until after the crash, when they ran a few blood tests on me.'

'You were on the pill?'

'Yes, I was.'

He sipped his coffee carefully, not meeting her eyes. 'Did you get sick? Is that what happened?'

She shook her head. 'I don't think so. I certainly never missed any.'

'It's never been one hundred percent effective.'

'There was a lot going on, Sam. We were very busy. I was working long shifts because one of our midwives was off ill and I was covering for her. One night we'd both had a lot of wine and…'

'It happened?'

She nodded. 'Yeah. It happened.'

Emily remembered that night so clearly. She had been exhausted, tired and upset. She hadn't seen Sam for almost three days. He'd been in surgery, or in and out of meetings, and they'd barely spoken. He certainly hadn't touched her for weeks. Their arguments had grown so awful that they hadn't talked in what felt like ages.

Emily had gone back to their house and, knowing she didn't have a shift the next day, had poured herself a large glass of wine. She'd almost finished it by the time Sam had arrived home, and something about him had seemed strange. He'd been different.

He'd said he was fed up with their fighting and that he missed her. She'd not let him say another word, had gone straight into his arms, and it had been as if someone had lit a fire. Suddenly everything had been urgent. They'd craved each other's bodies intensely and they'd made love on the carpet.

Afterwards he'd scooped her up in his arms and carried her to bed, where she'd fallen asleep. But when she'd woken in the morning he'd been gone again. It had been a brief truce, a cessation in their arguments, but when she'd sought him out to talk to him about what had happened he'd been too busy, and had answered her sharply, and before she'd known it they'd been arguing again.

It had been a difficult time for her. She'd been devastated, and then hopeful as she'd lain in his arms that they might be able to work things out—only to be dropped like a hot stone afterwards. Cast aside, feeling used.

Emily didn't want to tell him any of that. How could she? Here? In this beautiful city? Sam didn't need to hear any of that. He'd hate to hear it. He'd feel so guilty, and she didn't want him feeling that. They were here to deepen their love. Not go over old, painful ground which neither of them needed to return to.

She wanted them to be happy! She wanted the fairytale that she saw being played out every day. A happy family, a *loving* family, with everyone eager and excited about their pregnancy, planning nurseries and buying tiny clothes, getting excited about the approaching labour and thinking of names and choosing godparents. All of it.

She wanted a husband who was thrilled to be a father! She wanted the love that she'd never had. To give her child the stable family home that she had never experienced. There was no way she wanted to go back to the way they'd been before.

When she'd married Sam she'd made a commitment, and Emily believed you should always honour a commitment. If you had a child, you stuck around to love it and raise it. If you got married—well, you worked with the other person to make the marriage the best it could be. You didn't just give up when things got rough. You didn't just walk out because life seemed easier chasing another dream.

She looked down at the table. Sam still didn't know just *how bad* their arguments had been. How close she had come to leaving him. If he knew what they'd really been like…the amount of times she had stood in the shower and cried…

'I just want this trip to work so badly. I can't imagine how you must feel, having lost two years of your life. To wake up to this… I've tried to imagine what it would be like if it had happened to me.'

What if she *had* been the one with amnesia? If she thought he had just proposed and she had forgotten the wedding, the Grand Opening of their business. Their arguments? She would still feel blissfully happy after the proposal, right? Would she want to hear that she had threatened to leave him? Would she want to hear that they *weren't* the blissfully happy couple she believed them to be? Would she want to hear about some of the things they'd said to each other in the heat of the moment?

No.

'I'm okay.'

'Are you? Without memories of the opening of the birth centre, our wedding, our honeymoon...?'

'I can get all of that back.' He reached for her hand. 'Isn't that what you keep telling me? Isn't that why we're here?'

She nodded. It was. But getting his memories back was a double-edged sword. On the one hand he would have the joy of recalling all the good times they'd shared, but on the other...they could slip apart.

'Then let's work towards that. If I have any questions I'll ask you and you can answer. At least until my memories come back on their own. Okay?'

It would have to do. 'Okay.'

He smiled at her, his eyes glinting beneath the fairy lights.

The restaurant was beginning to get busy now, but they finished their coffees, paid and headed back out onto the street.

'Let's walk for a bit,' Sam suggested, draping an arm around her shoulder.

Paris at twilight was even more beautiful than it was during the day. There were still just as many people bustling about, and the roads were filled with cars and bikes, but everything seemed just that little bit calmer. As if everyone was more relaxed. Cafés and bistros poured out their lights and their aromatic scents into the streets, and they could hear conversation and muted laughter and people *enjoying* themselves. They passed a busker or two, food and flower stalls packing up for the day.

Sam bought her a single rose and presented it to her. 'For *madame*.'

'Thank you, kind sir.' She lifted the bloom to her nose and inhaled its soft sweet scent.

These were the moments that she'd yearned for. The last time they'd been in Paris Emily had been soaking up the atmosphere as much as Sam, but this time she knew it all a little better and so could concentrate more on enjoying being with Sam. Holding his hand. Being in his arms. Being in Paris itself was an added bonus.

Sam and Emily headed back over to the Seine and began to walk along its banks, arm in arm. It was a truce of sorts. Both of them were keen to make this trip work. To become close again.

They could hear accordion music in the distance, against the soft lapping of the water against the banks. A duck swam by, followed by a row of small ducklings, brown and yellow.

Emily sighed and looked about her. Couples sat on benches, hand in hand. Couples walked along the river, just like them. Couples sat on the stone steps, staring at the water. This really was a city meant for happiness. Not marital woes.

Sam kissed the side of her neck, inhaling the perfumed scent of her hair. He looked into her eyes. 'I'm sorry we've argued, and I'm sorry if I haven't been spending time with you. I guess you thought the same thing was happening again when I locked myself away in the office to catch up on things. Same old Sam, huh?'

She smiled. He was so unaware. So innocent

of how bad things had actually become. She wanted to make him feel better.

'That's okay. I know you feel the need to catch up. I would do the same thing in your shoes.'

'I'm so lucky to have you, Em.'

She smiled back at him.

The music was getting closer now, and they could see an old man, sitting on top of the stone steps with a genuine accordion. It wasn't a recording, or a CD playing, but a real, actual musician. He had an ancient face, but it was filled with passion as he played an old-style Argentinian tango, his fingers moving over the buttons and shaping the accordion with ease. Around him couples were dancing against the backdrop of the river. All ages, all abilities. It didn't matter. People were just being in the moment.

Sam and Emily watched for a second or two, and then Sam took her hand and led her into the group of dancers.

'Sam! What are you doing?' She laughed.

'We're going to dance!'

She laughed out loud in disbelief! Did Sam not remember? He'd done this the last time! It didn't seem as if he knew that.

But who cared? Emily wanted to dance with him. Their honeymoon had been the only time he had danced with her. Apart from at their wedding, of course, and she loved to dance.

At least she loved to dance with *him.*

The beautiful music was at once sudden and jarring, and had Sam pulling her up tight against his body. At first she laughed, embarrassed, but then she could see Sam smiling, taking the tango seriously, staring deeply into her eyes.

The Argentine tango was a dance made for eye contact and a close embrace. They moved as one. Forward. Back. To the side. Their steps were in tune with the music, first fast, then slow. Their bodies pressed together.

Slowly Emily began to forget that there were other couples dancing with them in the same space. All she concentrated on was Sam's eyes locked with her own. *Feeling* the pace and emotion of the music.

Being close to him. Held by him.

He had such piercing blue eyes. Intense. Moving. And they bored into her own with love and adoration as he twisted her this way, then that. The music began to get a little faster. He twisted her out to the side and she swept her foot out wide, as if scraping the floor, her skirt billowing out around her, before he pulled her back in close once again.

He really was a masterful dancer.

Why don't we do this more often?

She stared once again into his eyes as he pulled her close, making her gasp. This dance represented their relationship so easily. Passionate… tempestuous. Intimate.

She slid her leg up and down his, aware of the way he was breathing with her now in the dance, enjoying their closeness to each other. Aware of the way his body felt against hers.

Oh, how I've missed this man.

As the music built to its climax Sam spun them round in tight little movements and then, at the big finish, he dipped her backwards, bending over with her. As everyone began clapping to thank the musician he brought his face towards hers and kissed her deeply.

She fell into the kiss, draping her hands around his neck, unaware that the music had begun once again and the other couples were continuing to dance.

Straightening, they simply stood in the middle of the 'dance floor' and kissed.

Emily sank into him, claiming her husband back, claiming his mouth, his tongue, his taste. She wanted him so badly. Did he want her just as much? She hoped so. It had been so long since she had felt his touch upon her like this, so long since he had stared into her eyes like this, and she craved him like a drug.

As the kiss ended they continued to stare into each other's eyes. For a moment neither of them said anything, and then she felt Sam slip his fingers into hers.

'Let's go back to the hotel.'

She nodded, understanding his intent, and together they left the dancing group.

CHAPTER FIVE

NEITHER OF THEM said anything on the way back to the hotel. They walked with purpose, through the evening light, and in their hotel room, surrounded once again by luxury, Emily suddenly realised just how much of a long day they'd had—the flight, the taxi ride, dinner, exploring Paris, and then telling Sam how bad things really were.

She felt she wanted to refresh herself. Wash away the travel. Take a few moments to prepare herself for this. They hadn't been intimate for such a long time and she wanted it to be perfect.

'I'm going to take a shower.'

Sam nodded.

Inside the shower room, Emily turned on the hot spray and removed her clothes. Stepping beneath the powerful refreshing water, she gasped at the feel of it on the back of her neck before turning around to face the water and look for soap.

That was when she became aware of the fact that Sam had joined her. She heard the glass shower door open and then sensed his presence.

Smiling to herself, she sighed in delight as she felt Sam's hands slide over the skin around her hips, before he slid them over her belly and pulled her back against him.

Emily closed her eyes with pure elation. She could feel him. Every familiar inch of him. His hands sliding over her breasts...his fingers splaying as they rubbed over her sensitive nipples. Leaning back into him, she allowed herself to enjoy the moment as his lips caressed her neck. She had not felt his touch for so long! *Too* long.

The last time Sam had joined her in the shower had been in this very shower, on their honeymoon. They'd just come back from visiting the top of the Eiffel Tower, watching the city from its viewing platforms and taking photographs. They'd hired bicycles and cycled around Paris in the midday heat, and by the end of the day they'd both been sweaty and tired. They'd fallen into the shower cubicle with giggles and laughter, holding onto each other as they kissed each other and covered each other in foam, their limbs sliding over each other.

Here they stood once again.

It gave Emily a strange sense of *déjà-vu*. Shivering, she closed her eyes as Sam's hands once again sought her peaked nipples. The heat and spray of the water, the feel of his fingers upon her, the way he kissed and nipped the skin on her neck and collarbone, his lips brushing like feathers…it was utterly delightful.

'Oh, Sam…'

He turned her to him and cupped her face, bringing her lips to his.

Oh, I've missed his touch…

A few weeks ago she could never have dreamed that they would be like this. She'd stood over a suitcase, planning to leave him! She'd felt angry at him, frustrated that he would never talk to her, or allow her to explain how she was feeling. He'd never listened—he'd ignored her, stayed away.

She'd never believed she would have *this* again.

Those days she'd spent worrying about what would happen when he woke from his coma had been swept away by the realisation that Sam couldn't remember the last two years. That, for him, their relationship was in a totally different place. And the baby! He'd not reacted badly to the news either—which she didn't want to think about. Didn't want to question.

All that mattered was the touch of his hands upon her, the feel of his arousal against her, the clear signs that he wanted *her*, wanted the baby, that he was happy despite his memory loss. And that they were reconnecting.

We can get through this. We can do it together.

A wave of tiredness swept over her, but she pushed it away. All these hours they'd spent awake—the travelling, the waiting in the airport, the long day. Her exhaustion was catching up with her, but she couldn't let it overwhelm her. She had waited for this moment with Sam. Had craved this intimacy between them. Something which had been sadly lacking for too long.

How many nights had she lain awake in bed, waiting for him to come home? Waiting for him to come to bed just so she could feel the security of him next to her on the mattress even if he did turn his back?

Too many times.

How many times had he stayed away? How

many times had he left her wondering where he was actually sleeping? So she'd had to go tiptoeing through the house at night until she found the room that he was in?

Too many to count.

How did she know whether he would do it to her again? It had to be in him, didn't it? The rejection of her. The rejection of the baby. Even if it wasn't in him now it was *part of him*. He had already done it to her. He just couldn't remember. When would it start? Was it already brewing? Was he already having secret thoughts that he was holding back? What if he used her right now and then in the morning cast her aside?

Feeling afraid and confused, Emily turned her back to him. She needed a moment. To think. To *breathe*.

Sam ran his fingers through her long wet hair and reached past her for a shampoo bottle. Squirting some into his hands, he began to stroke it into her long locks, gently massaging her scalp, making sure he touched every strand, every length, trying to make the experience pleasurable for her.

She pressed her hands against the wall of the

shower cubicle and gave in to the massage. It felt so good to be loved by Sam again. Cherished. But she wasn't sure what she should be thinking. Should she just enjoy what he was initiating? Or turn and tell him the full truth? Take the bull by its very sharp, pointed horns and tell him everything?

Emily pressed her hands against the tiled wall, feeling its reassuring, very solid presence.

I can't. I'd risk everything. It's best he doesn't know I was going to leave him.

The head massage was soothing. Too soothing. She felt as if she might almost drop off to sleep, it was so nice.

Emily held her head under the shower so that the shampoo would be washed away. The hot suds ran down her body, trailed by Sam's hands, his fingertips, a feather touch down her back, over the swell of her hips and bottom and the sides of her thighs.

Then he was reaching past her for conditioner, and as he smoothed on the cold creamy hair product, smoothing it down the hair that almost fell to her waist, she let out a long sigh of pleasure.

She dipped her head under the spray once more, then turned to him. The heat within the shower was becoming too much. 'I need to get out. Cool down.'

He kissed her shoulder. 'I won't be a minute. Get into bed. I'll join you soon.'

Emily stepped out and grabbed a large fluffy bath towel, which she wrapped herself in, and then left the steamy shower room.

The hotel suite felt much cooler, and it was as if there was more air. Breathing more easily, she removed the towel and rubbed at her long hair, then padded across the suite in her bare feet towards the bed. She smiled as she slipped beneath the covers.

Tonight she would reclaim her husband.

Tonight she would get him back for good.

Sam turned off the shower and grabbed a towel to wrap around his waist and another to rub at his wet hair.

The shower had felt good. But it was even better to have shared it with Em. It was time for them to grow close—especially as he'd spent the last few days stuck in his office at the house, trying to catch up on all the paperwork that had accrued in his absence. Trying to look at business growth charts and financial losses, turnover and profit, stock ordering systems and staff training reports, and all the other reams of paper that had just seemed to grow out of nowhere and had almost brought on a headache.

Two years' worth of catching up had caused him to fall asleep there more than once! He felt sure that Em wasn't approving of that, but she hadn't complained. Not really. She'd given him a worried look or two, whenever she'd popped in with a coffee, or to say goodnight, but that was to be expected after his accident.

Now they were in Paris, and for him it felt like the first time. Sitting across from Em in that restaurant and seeing the love in her eyes for him had warmed his heart. And then later, when they'd danced together, it had been clear they hadn't touched for an age, and it had been painfully exquisite to take her in his arms once more and see the hope and elation in her eyes.

He was eager for them to improve their relationship. To find the marriage they'd had at the beginning, before the arguments had started.

They'd been good together once, but hearing how he'd been with her had rung too true. He could imagine himself trying to avoid the question about having babies—could picture himself staying away, thinking that if he did that at least then they wouldn't be arguing. That somehow he'd be trying to save her from pain.

Sam threw the towel he'd been drying his hair with to the floor and stepped out of the shower room. He'd only kept her waiting for a few minutes—he felt sure she wouldn't have minded.

Em lay in the bed, her naked back to him, her still drying hair spread out over the pillow.

Smiling, he lifted the covers, removed the towel from his waist and slid in next to her, his hand roving over her naked hip and around her thigh.

'Hello again, gorgeous…'

He waited for an answer, and when he didn't get one he propped himself up in bed and peered over at her face.

Was she *asleep*?

'Em?' he whispered. *'Em?'*

She breathed steadily, her eyes closed, her face in a truly relaxed state.

She's exhausted! Must be all those hormones...

His hand resting on her belly stilled. There was a slight—ever so slight—roundness to it that hadn't been there before.

Our baby.

Sam laid his head down onto the pillow as he spooned his wife. How would he deal with what was to come? Could he do it? He'd have to, wouldn't he? The baby was already happening. Already growing within her.

He wasn't surprised that he'd not been able to find a way to tell her about Serena. He had always kept that part of him close. Tightly boxed away, never to be shown the light. But perhaps by doing that—by not telling Em—he had caused a different rift. One he could never fix. He hoped not. He hoped that there was still happiness ahead for them both. Perhaps he could find a way to tell her about his baby sister?

Sam swallowed hard. *I'm not sure I can.* He'd spoken about it to nobody. Even his own family didn't talk about it to each other. He'd learnt that from them. You take the hurt, you stamp it down and you bury it—bury it deep, where no one will ever see it. You don't mention the disturbed soil, you don't mention the empty crib, you don't say anything when you see someone crying. You stay away from all of that.

It had worked for him thus far, hadn't it?

No. Your wife was miserable!

He would have to hope this trip would give him time. Time to find a way through his concerns and fears about being a good, protective father.

Because it was real. The baby was in there, growing. He had seen it on the scan and it had taken his breath away.

Maybe a son. Maybe a daughter. Like Serena. If it was a girl, would he ever truly relax? Would he stand watch over her every night? Checking her breathing? Checking she was still okay?

Was that even possible? Not twenty-four hours a day. But how *could* he keep his baby safe? If something happened to their child Emily would be distraught! She might blame him.

And if it were a boy? Would he be any more relaxed? *No.* He supposed they could get a baby monitor that alerted you to your baby's breathing. He supposed he could get a camera for the baby's room, too. But would any of that make him feel better?

Sam wasn't sure. But what he *did* know was that they were against the clock. He had six months to get his head around this. Six months either to accept what was happening and get on with it, or…or what?

Sam cradled his wife's abdomen. The baby was safe for now.

He could only hope that it would stay that way. And they were making inroads in their marriage too. Coming here. Spending time together away from work. But there was work to do here too… on their marriage.

It took some time, but eventually he fell asleep, his eyes finally closing on the shadows crossing the room and the constant glow of light touching the ceiling, coming from the Eiffel Tower…

'Let's hire some bikes,' Sam suggested, a big smile on his face.

Indulgently, Emily smiled back, tearing a piece from her croissant as they breakfasted alfresco on their hotel suite balcony. It was a beautiful summer morning and she'd had an excellent night's sleep, waking to find herself snuggled into Sam's warm, inviting body.

'We did that the last time. And I don't want to get exhausted again.'

Em felt terrible for having fallen asleep last night. They'd both been expecting to *become more acquainted*, and yet the second she'd lain her head upon the pillow she'd gone off to the Land of Nod. Waking this morning to see the sunlight streaming through the windows, and having a distinctly empty memory of any recent lovemaking, had made her feel incredibly embarrassed and awkward. She'd slipped out of his arms and gone outside to the balcony.

'I meant those little moped things. I heard someone say yesterday that they rode around Montmartre and had an amazing time. Let's do that. No energy required.'

The buttery croissant was light and fluffy in her mouth and she swallowed it whilst smearing another piece with jam. 'Okay…sounds fun. What do you want to do in Montmartre?'

'Whatever takes our fancy. Let's just ride around and explore.'

'Okay.'

It sounded a great idea. They hadn't done *that* before, and she relished the idea of finding somewhere new to explore together. They needed to spend time like that. Who knew what might trigger his memory? Why not try something different?

'It's going to be another lovely summer's day.'

'It's always a lovely summer's day when I'm with you.'

She smiled. 'Ditto.'

'I'm going to get dressed. You enjoy breakfast. You need your strength. Don't want you flaking out on me.'

The croissant went dry in her mouth and guilt made the breakfast suddenly unpalatable. She hadn't meant to fall asleep last night, but the second she'd got into the bed she'd relaxed and closed her eyes for just a moment…

Sam must have felt so disappointed when he'd got out of the shower and found her fast asleep. Yet he was being so gentlemanly by not mentioning it.

But what could she do? It was done now, and he was obviously trying hard to not focus on it.

She should do the same thing, too, and get ready for their day in Montmartre.

When she went into the bedroom she gasped to see a box upon the bed, tied with a bow. 'What's that?'

'Open it.' Sam grinned.

Puzzled, she sat on the bed and untied the bow, sliding off the ribbon before opening the box. Whatever was inside was wrapped in pale pink tissue paper, and when she opened that she gasped out loud. 'Oh, my goodness! When did you get this?'

Inside the box was the beautiful powder-blue dress that she'd spotted in the airport shop when they'd passed by at Charles de Gaulle. She'd pointed it out to him, had oohed and aahed at the dress in the window, but they'd hurried on, eager to get to their destination.

How had Sam arranged this?

'Sam…'

'I couldn't resist. I know it probably won't fit you in a few more weeks, but… I wanted you to have it.'

She stood up and draped it against her, checking herself in the mirror. 'I love it, Sam—thank you. I'm going to wear it today.'

'On a moped? Why not wear it tonight, when we get back? We could go out for a meal.'

She nodded. 'Perfect. Thank you.'

'You're worth it. I love you.'

She stroked his face, loving this side of Sam. 'I love you, too.'

He grinned. 'Okay. Get dressed and let's get ready to ride!'

At first Emily wasn't too good at riding the moped. But after a few false starts, where she kangarooed along the road, and a bit of extra tuition from a patient Sam, they finally got going and rode through the city, out towards Montmartre.

They stopped and parked on the Rue Jardieu, to get off and have a good look around the area, famed for its street painters and artists. They walked towards the Square Willette and gasped in awe at the sight of the Basilica de Sacré-Coeur—the beautiful, pure white Byzantine church that looked down the hill at them as if surveying all that it could see.

'That's just beautiful, isn't it, Sam?'

'It is. Should we go take a look around?'

She nodded.

They took their time—walking through the square, then up the terraced stairs, past a musician playing the harp, to whom they gave a few coins—and finally they stood in front of the wonderful, imposing building.

There were three arches, and above them bronze statues of a saint and a king, welcoming them in, After taking a photo or two, they stepped inside, into the cool interior.

The beautiful three-domed church was lit by dozens of stained glass windows, surrounding the building, and they walked around quietly, respecting their reverent surroundings.

Emily felt the need to slip her hand into Sam's, and she watched as Sam stopped to light a candle and stood back to stare at it, as if in contemplation.

She frowned, wondering who the candle was for. Sam still had both his parents and all five of his siblings. Was it for a grandparent? It seemed a strange thing for him to do, and she wondered about the Sam that she didn't know. There had to be something. Back in his past. And it was something he clearly hadn't forgotten about after his accident. An old memory? An old pain?

She knew Sam had secrets, and it had always pained her that he'd never chosen to share those with her. *Why* hadn't he? Was it because of the arguments, the distance between them? Why hadn't he told her about them when they *weren't* arguing? He'd had time. They talked to each other about most things back then. It hurt to think that he was keeping part of himself hidden, that he didn't trust her.

But she couldn't ask him here. Not with all these people around. She decided to wait until they were out of the church, maybe having lunch, and then she would ask him.

Watching Sam made her realise that she didn't have anyone to light a candle for. As far as she knew her mother was still alive. Her Aunt Sylvia and her Uncle Martin were too. No one had any idea who her father was. Grandparents? She had no recollection. So Emily had no need to make such a beautiful acknowledgement. It made her feel a little rootless, not knowing more about her mother and her family. As if a part of her was missing. That she was somehow incomplete. It was why she had fought so hard to save her marriage. She couldn't lose Sam, too. She would feel so lost.

They continued to look around, then eventually emerged outside, walking back around to the front steps and looking out over the city.

'It was so peaceful in there, wasn't it?' he asked.

Emily nodded. 'It was. Very.' She looked at his face for a moment, wondering whether *now* would be a good time to ask about the candle, but she saw a shadow cross his face and decided against it. Not yet. There would be a time and place soon, though.

'Where do you think we should go next?'

'I'm not sure. Should we go back and grab the mopeds? Ride around?'

She nodded. The bikes would be good. Sam's mood had changed in the basilica, and she wanted to see the joyful Sam she had witnessed that morning. This was meant to be fun, and yet they had descended into a sombre mood.

They walked back through the square, enjoying the wide expanses of grass and the flowers, the singing of the birds in the trees, until they got back to their mopeds and donned their helmets.

Their engines roared into life and they set off into the small, winding streets, looking for treasures.

It came suddenly and without warning. Sam was riding his moped, following Emily. He'd been watching the traffic, enjoying the sight of his wife's hair billowing behind her, and the memory came from nowhere.

Emily striding away from him in a hospital corridor, anger pouring from every part of her body. Stiff shoulders. Purposeful.

He called her name in exasperation. 'Emily!'

She stopped walking. Turned and her face was full of tears. Her eyes red and streaming...

Sam blinked and a car sounded its horn at him as he wavered slightly. Straightening his bike, he raised his hand in apology to the driver.

What the hell had that been?

The hospital corridor had been at the Monterey. He'd recognised it. It had been the corridor leading to Emily's office, because there'd been that picture on the wall. The watercolour of a pixie gazing at her reflection in a pool. Em had picked it out from an exhibition she'd seen.

In the memory his wife had been upset. Vastly upset. With him. *At him?*

What had happened next?

He cursed to himself, angry that the memory had been fleeting and brief. But then, strangely, his heart began to pound as he realised another memory had returned! Bad as it had been—*again*—a memory *had* returned!

Was this going to be it? Were they about to start coming back?

Should he mention it to Emily?

He pondered over that. If he told her he'd experienced another flash of memory she'd want to know what it was, and if he told her… Well, she might not want another bad memory being dragged up. Not here. Not on this holiday. She'd wanted them to enjoy this place. They were both hoping this trip to Paris would bring them closer again.

But hadn't she been the one to suggest that Paris would be the place for him to regain his memories?

This was what they were here for, after all. And, even though it was a bad memory, perhaps it seemed worse than it really was? Perhaps it was something that could be easily explained and Emily would laugh about it and tell him it was nothing?

Sam was desperate to get his memories back, and the fleeting one he'd just experienced enticed him to believe that others were there, waiting for him to claim them. If he explored this memory with Emily then it might cause others to come through.

He had to take that chance.

After they'd been driving around for a while Emily pointed over at what looked like a vast marketplace but was in fact a square, full of artists and portraitists, all sitting beneath large red umbrellas to protect themselves and their work from the sun or occasional inclement weather. The square was filled with laughter and French voices. Tourists and locals milled around, taking photographs or sitting for paintings beneath an avenue of leafy green trees.

Ahead of him, Emily removed her helmet, shaking out her hair, and slipped on her sunglasses. 'This looks great, Sam! Shall we get our picture painted?'

He loved her enthusiasm. Loved her smile. He didn't want to lose that. He decided to tell her about the memory later—perhaps when they were sitting for the picture.

'Okay.'

They locked up their mopeds, pocketing the keys, and headed into the bustling square.

There were some amazing artists there, using a vast array of techniques—acrylics, watercolour, pencil, paste, chalk. If there was a way of putting a picture onto paper or canvas, then it was here. And he knew Emily loved art.

They took their time looking about, trying to find someone they thought might capture the two of them perfectly, and stopped when they saw a caricaturist.

'Oh, this will be fun, Sam. Let's ask this one.'

Thankfully the artist spoke English, and they negotiated a price before they sat down together and smiled at the artist who soon set to work.

'You are here on holiday?' the artist asked.

Emily smiled at him. 'Sort of a second honeymoon. It's a long story,' she explained.

'Ah, *voyage de noces. La lune de miel.*'

'That sounds beautiful.'

The artist smiled. 'It is meant to be. *C'est romantique!*'

Emily and Sam shared an odd smile. The painter obviously saw them as a couple, very much in love, and only they knew the real truth.

As the artist worked, concentrating on his drawing whilst occasionally peering around his easel at the two of them, Sam decided to let Emily know what had happened.

'You know, Em… I think whilst we were riding here I remembered something.' He glanced at her to see her reaction and noticed with alarm that she seemed to freeze, pausing for a brief millisecond as if in fear, before she let out a breath and smiled.

'You did? What?'

He shook his head. 'It was brief. Barely anything, really. We were at the Monterey, heading for your office, but…'

She looked curious. 'But?'

'You were walking away from me, and when I called your name you turned around and you were crying.'

Emily looked away from him, frowning.

Was she trying to remember the incident? Had it been a common occurrence? He knew they'd been arguing.

'I see.'

'What was that about?'

Em shook her head. 'It's not important.'

'It is,' he pressed on. 'I need to understand what was going on if we're to make this work.'

She looked down at the ground. 'If it's the argument I remember, then I'd tried to track you down at work because you hadn't been home that night. I wanted to know where you'd been.'

He stared at her, afraid of her answer. 'And?'

'You'd been out wining and dining clients, and I was annoyed because you were spending so much time wooing other people that you never had time for me.'

'I see.'

'I wasn't being selfish, Sam. I hadn't seen you for what felt like days! I'd been worried about you. Worried about *us*. I'd spent hours huddled on the couch, afraid of what might have happened, and then I learnt that you'd been out having a good time.'

He looked away. 'Oh.'

'So I was hurt and angry and I stormed away from you.'

Sam almost didn't want to believe it. But he could imagine himself doing that. Avoiding the main argument and throwing himself into something else instead, hoping that if he just never talked about the thing that bothered him then it wouldn't bother anyone else. It was what he had been taught to do.

'So your memories are starting to come back?'

He gazed at her and he could see that she was sad. But there was something else in her eyes that he couldn't fathom. What was it? She was looking at him as if…as if she was afraid.

No. That couldn't be true. Why would Emily be afraid of his memories returning? She *wanted* them to. It couldn't be fear. There was no need for it. She'd already told him how bad it had become between them. For that he was grateful. It would have been so easy for her to say that they'd been getting on fine. He had to be wrong—it couldn't have been fear that he'd seen.

Shaking his head, he decided to forget about it. The artist obviously thought they were happy, because when he showed them the picture—the two of them beneath a backdrop of the Eiffel Tower—he had drawn red hearts blossoming all around them.

Sam wondered briefly how the artist might have painted them if he'd known the truth? Would they have had blindfolds over their eyes? Hands clamped over their mouths?

He solemnly wished their lives were truly like the caricature.

They decided to walk through some of the streets, snapping pictures of things they found interesting. They found a very pretty vineyard—which seemed an odd thing to find amongst a bustling mass of streets—then a street of nineteenth-century villas and gardens which were in full bloom, and in another a windmill.

Montmartre was a place of contrasts, it seemed, and they could understand why it had once been *the* place to be seen if you were an artist or a painter.

'We ought to get something to eat,' Emily said, rubbing at her stomach. 'I'm getting very hungry with all this exploring.'

'What do you fancy?'

'Something quick.'

They found a small stall selling pitta pockets stuffed with a choice of chicken, beef or vegetables, served with plantains, avocado or black beans. They both chose a chicken pitta with plantain chips and two cold limeades.

'Oh, my goodness, that's delightful,' Emily said, savouring her sandwich and using her fingers to capture a piece of chicken.

'Something new for you?'

She nodded, smiling, her mouth full.

Sam smiled back. The food was indeed delicious, and he realised that he was loving today. Loving making these new memories with Em after the regret of knowing he had missed so much and that some of what he had missed had been awful. But he was determined to be positive and to look forward. He had a business that by all accounts was doing well, a gorgeous, wonderful wife whom he loved with his entire heart, and they were trying their best to tackle their problems the best they knew how.

And he was going to be a father.

That in itself was a scary thing to admit to

himself, and he'd tried to put it in the 'positive' category but he couldn't. It was not something that he could escape from. He had to face it. Head-on. No matter if he had doubts.

Em took a thoughtful nibble of her pitta. 'This morning, Sam…back in the basilica…you lit a candle.'

He glanced at her, acknowledging her statement with a nod.

'Who was it for?'

So she definitely didn't know, then. He obviously hadn't told her about Serena. He supposed he knew why. He'd always kept that part of himself hidden. Had shared it with no one. And when Emily had brought up the idea of having a baby in the past he must have dug his heels in even more.

Was this the root of all their problems? His refusal to talk about his deepest, darkest secret? Had it been his fault all along? Hurting Emily by pushing her away? Causing her grief by refusing even to discuss something that was so important? It must have made her feel tiny. Belittled. She was his wife and he wouldn't even talk to her about what ailed him.

But did he want her to find out about it *here*? When they were trying to make new happy memories for themselves?

'It was for us. A candle to show the way.'

She smiled, relieved, and laid her head upon his shoulder. 'That's so sweet. For us? Thank you, Sam.'

Pressing down against the guilt he felt at lying to her, he kissed the side of her face, and he was just about to take another bite of his sandwich when something happened that seemed almost to occur in slow motion.

He looked out across the street and spotted an old man, looking for a place to cross. The road wasn't too busy, but there was a steady stream of traffic coming both ways. The side where the old man stood was clear, and he began to amble across. But halfway he spotted a motorbike, tried to hurry, then tripped—just before the motorbike collided with him.

Sam dropped his pitta pocket as the motorcyclist was thrown through the air and the old man crashed to the ground, spinning round from the impact.

His hands, frantically trying to control the steering wheel...

'Oh, my God, Sam!' Emily gripped his arm.

He was up. Dashing across the road, calling out, 'Call an ambulance! *Appelez une ambulance!*'

The rest of the traffic drew to a halt, drivers and passengers getting out to look at the crash.

The motorcyclist had been thrown clear and had rolled across the road. He was struggling to get up.

Sam ran to the old man first, who was lying motionless on the ground, with a wound on his head, bleeding profusely, his elbows and arms torn, his leg at a painful angle.

But he was breathing.

'Lie still! Don't move.' The man's eyes fluttered open as he came back to consciousness. 'Stop—*arretez*—don't move,' Sam ordered, holding the man's neck still to maintain his c-spine control. He glanced up and over at Emily. 'Check the other one!'

He watched as Emily hurried over to check the motorcyclist, who had now sat up and was trying to remove his helmet.

'No—*non*! Keep it on!' he heard her say.

The old man began to groan.

'What's your name? *Comment vous appelez-vous?*'

More groans, then, 'Alain…'

'Alain, do you speak English? *Parlez-vous Anglais?*'

Alain tried to nod, but Sam kept his head steady. 'Stay still, my friend. I'm a doctor. You must keep still—you've been hurt.'

Sam had never felt so useless in his life. He had no medical equipment with him here. He had nothing! How could he help this man and take care of him without the back-up of his team? And he wasn't an ER specialist. He dealt with labouring women. Not elderly men hurt in road traffic accidents.

Emily came running over. 'The motorcyclist is all right. His leathers and his helmet protected him, and he wasn't going fast.'

It was a pity the same could not be said for Alain. The old man was very thin and very frail. He'd probably broken a lot of bones.

'Hold his head for me. That's it. Alain? This is

my wife, Emily. Lie still for her and I'm going to check you over.'

He grabbed at his own shirt and tore off a strip, folding it and pressing it tightly against Alain's bleeding head.

Sam started checking Alain for breaks. His collarbone seemed fractured, maybe a rib or two. His right arm probably. His pelvis? To be on the safe side Sam removed his leather belt and fed it under Alain's waist, looping it over and pulling it tight to secure the pelvic basin just in case. A bleed from a break there could be disastrous. His lower leg was certainly fractured.

'Alain? Where does it hurt?'

'Partout...'

Everywhere. He wasn't surprised. He'd been hit by a motorbike. How fast had it been travelling? Forty kilometres per hour? Maybe a little less? It was hard to tell.

In the distance he could hear sirens approaching. 'Help's coming, Alain. Do you have any health conditions I should know about? Any allergies?'

'Non...'

'Okay, *c'est bon*. Anyone we can call for you? Your wife? Family?'

'*Ma femme*... Celine...'

'Okay, what's her number?'

Sam listened and wrote down the telephone number Alain gave. He could hand all this information over to the ambulance crew.

'You're doing well, Alain. A few broken bones and a head wound, but I think you're going to be okay. The ambulance is coming.'

'*Merci*...'

Sam looked at the motorcyclist. He did indeed appear to be okay, which was good news, but he would still need to be checked over in hospital. He stood behind them, a stream of French words falling steadily from his mouth. Sam couldn't catch it all, but he thought the man was trying to say he had not seen Alain until the last minute.

Well, that was something for the police to sort out.

He felt a moment of fear. Had this happened at *their* accident site? Had people got out of their cars and stood watching as assistance was given? Had people gazed at *his* injured head, too?

Sam needed to keep Alain stable. The main thing was that he was conscious and breathing.

An ambulance fought its way through the traffic and pulled to a halt a few yards from them. It didn't take too long for Sam to feed back to the crew what he'd seen happen and his assessment of Alain.

He stood back as they took over, fitting a proper brace to Alain's pelvis and returning Sam's belt, giving their patient oxygen, fitting a neck brace and loading him into the ambulance.

As they drove away Sam stood on the path looking after them, his arm around Emily. 'You okay, Em?'

'I'm fine. Are you? You look terrible…your poor shirt…'

'It's nothing. It's Alain I feel sorry for. Poor guy, lying on the road like that.' He turned to look at her. 'Made me think about what happened to us…'

She swallowed hard. 'We survived. So will Alain.'

'I hope so. I gave the crew my number. They promised they would ring with an update when they could.'

'You did all you could have done.'

He shook his head. 'It happened so fast…and yet I could see it about to happen, like it was in slow motion, like it triggered—' He stopped talking. Went silent.

Emily looked up at him. 'Triggered what? A memory?'

'I don't know. I need to think about it. But I think I saw…'

She looked scared. 'Saw what?'

'I think I saw *our* crash. I think I saw me spinning the wheel. I don't know…'

Emily laid a hand upon his arm. 'I think we need a strong coffee or two. Let's go find a café.'

He looked at her and nodded. That seemed sensible. He didn't want them to get onto the mopeds right after seeing that bike accident. He wouldn't feel right. And it had made him see how vulnerable Emily was, exposed like that on the bike. Anything could hit her. Could take her from him!

He couldn't have that.

'Good idea.' He resolved to get the mopeds returned as soon as possible.

CHAPTER SIX

THE COFFEE WENT some way to restoring their nerves. As did the slice of caramel *dacquoise* they shared. And once they'd returned the mopeds, and Sam had changed into a new shirt at the hotel, throwing his torn one into the wastepaper basket, they decided to head back out and reclaim the day for their own.

Em held his hand as they walked. 'So that's a couple of memories that have come back since we've been here. That's good.'

That day he'd followed her to her office at the hospital, after they'd argued about him partying, had been the day he'd accused her of being selfish, of only thinking of herself and what she wanted from their relationship.

'Selfish? You think I'm selfish because I want to start a family with you?'

'It's all you ever talk about! "I want to get

pregnant..." "I want a baby..." "I want us to start trying." Do you ever ask me what I want?'

She'd shaken her head, confused.

'What do *you want, Sam?'*

He'd straightened, his face blanching.

'I'm not ready to be a father yet.'

'Why? Please tell me.'

'I can't...'

His voice had trailed away, and for a moment he'd looked helpless and lost. She'd feared, then, that he was unable to tell her something painful, so she'd broached the subject herself.

'Don't you love me, Sam?'

'Of course I do.'

'Then why don't you want us to have a child together? I don't understand. What's so wrong with starting a family? We help everyone else do it, day after day, why not us?'

He'd not answered her and so, frustrated, she'd stormed away from him, furious that she could never get a straight answer from him, furious with herself for allowing it to mean so much that it was tearing them apart.

She'd told him earlier today that she'd just been upset at him for staying out with those clients.

Well, it had certainly been more than that. Sam hadn't come home that night but had worked straight through, and he'd only gone off shift when she'd clocked on in the morning.

It had been so humiliating! All the staff at the Monterey must have noticed. How could they not? They'd raised their voices in the hospital corridor and brought a personal matter into the workplace. Even Emily was appalled at herself for that. What must the patients have thought? A premier birthing centre set in the heart of a marital dispute!

Keen to put good memories back into Sam's head, Emily decided it was time for them to return to the Île de Reuily, otherwise known as the Temple of Love. They'd gone there on their first trip, and Emily was keen for them to go again. There was so much they needed to talk about and sort through, and now that his memories might be coming back she was keen to let him know and understand exactly where she had been coming from. Before any more came back and completely blindsided him. Damaging them for ever.

They needed to talk about the family issue.

About what had been keeping them separate. It had to be confronted—probably here more than anywhere, because they were now in a place where *both of them* were trying to save their marriage.

The distance between them had been scaring her. She'd known their marriage was failing, and yet every time she'd tried to get Sam back he'd just moved farther and farther away. She'd not known who he was any more, and it had made her fear that she'd never really known him at all.

This man had made her world shine brighter once and she wanted that back again. There had to be a way for them to get there.

Sam knew a little of her background, but she'd never gone into detail. Nor had he. Their relationship had blossomed quickly and ferociously. Both of them had been swept away on an intense new love, and if they hadn't been busy planning their wedding they'd been busy planning and running their business.

They needed this trip to get to know one another properly. Away from work. On neutral ground. They needed to understand each other—who they were and what had made them that way. Maybe then, and only then, would they begin to understand where it had all gone wrong.

So when Sam had returned to their room to change his shirt Emily had picked up the full picnic basket she'd asked the hotel to provide. The temple would be the perfect spot for them to talk, to clear the air and to watch the sun set.

'Where are we going?' Sam asked.

'On a magical mystery tour. Trust me.' She smiled, making her way to the Line Eight Métro to get to their destination.

They people-watched for a while. Paris was filled with so many unique faces, both residents and visitors, but the city had a certain style, a *je ne sais quois* that oozed from every pore, every street, and the mix of cultures and voices helped provide that.

At the Michel Bizot stop they got off and began their walk up a long palm-tree-lined avenue. The weather was beautiful. Perfect for a picnic. Emily was looking forward to sitting down with him, enjoying his company with the good food that the hotel had provided.

They stopped briefly to look and take photos at the Musée National de l'Histoire de l'Immigration.

It was a magnificent building that had figures and animals, trees and historic events carved into its exterior, like a stone Bayeux tapestry. Intrigued, they headed inside, and Sam asked if they could leave their picnic basket at Reception whilst they took a look around.

It was the perfect place to revive their sense of wellbeing after the accident they'd witnessed, and as they were looking around Sam received a call from the hospital to inform him that Alain was stable. Happy at the news, Sam draped his arm around Emily's shoulder and they walked around the numerous eclectic displays.

'I could spend all day here,' Emily said, knowing that they wouldn't. Knowing that she needed to talk to him. Confront him about the real issue. But for now she could pretend that all of that wasn't ahead of her. At least she could try to.

'Why don't we? There's a park nearby—we could eat the picnic there afterwards.'

She thought about it, but, no, she wanted them to go to the temple on the island. 'I really want to show you the lake and island I was telling you about.'

She didn't want him to know why. Yes, it

was the most beautiful place she'd ever been, but it was also isolated. The perfect place for them to talk. To share. To make up some of the ground between them, to forge new bonds and strengthen themselves once again. At least that was what she hoped would happen. But it was nerve-racking. What if it all went wrong? What if he refused to talk about his past? His issues?

He nodded, seeming happy to be guided by her. Paris had been her plan, after all, and so far it was working. He'd gained a few memories that he hadn't had before.

After an hour or two spent in the museum, they headed into the park of the Bois de Vincennes.

There was an exquisite flower garden, a kaleidoscope of colour, surrounded by neat swathes of pale green lawn and dark green trees, and with the heat of the summer sun it was the ideal place for them to be after their adventure that morning.

Emily smiled as Sam looked around, bowled over by the beauty of the place. 'I told you it was worth it.'

He turned to face her. '*You're* worth it.'

She smiled back and kissed him, revelling in the taste of his lips, the sun on their faces. In the warmth of not just being with the man she loved, but the joy of knowing that she was getting back the husband she adored. That he was trying as much as she was.

But nerves were bubbling under the surface. It was nearly time. Time to say everything. Explain everything. Dig deep and find out what had truly been keeping them apart.

Where would they both be by the end of this day? A little closer? Understanding each other? Or would they be even further apart?

'Let's head for the lake. I hope you've got your arms ready to do some rowing?'

He nodded. 'I've carried this basket most of the afternoon. I'm sure my muscles are all warmed up for the oars.'

There was a long row of boats lined up by the lakeside.

'They've all got names on. I wonder if there's a rowing boat called *Emily*?'

'Or *Sam*. Not all boats are named after ladies, you know?'

The white boats were small, edged in red,

with the inside of the boat painted in blue. Once they'd paid and Sam had helped Emily get in, making sure she was sitting down properly before he began, he took hold of the oars and gently pushed them out onto the lake.

It was very calm on the water. Poplars and tall grass bordered the lake, whilst weeping willows dipped their weary branches down into the water, creating little concealed areas where couples could take a boat and have a little privacy if they so wished.

But Emily knew exactly where she wanted to go.

There were hardly any other people out on the lake as she pointed across the still green water to the island in the centre. Upon the island stood a beautiful domed temple, supported by tall, slim columns of white stone. It sat on a grassy outcrop, and beneath it could be seen craggy rocks and what looked like, from a distance, numerous caves.

'Is that where we're headed?' asked Sam.

She nodded. 'It is. It's the place you first called me Mrs Saint.'

'Oh, yes? What else did I say to you there?'

She laughed. 'Lots of things! Some of them rather rude…'

'I'm intrigued!'

'Feels odd to think that we're back here and this time I'm carrying our baby.'

He glanced at her briefly, then looked behind him at the temple once more.

Sensing a shift in his mood, Emily tilted her head in question. 'Are you happy, Sam?'

He turned back to her. 'Me? Course I am. How could I not be? I'm here in Paris, with my beautiful wife, on a gorgeous day, and…' His voice trailed away.

'And…?'

'And I couldn't be any happier.'

'Really? You seem a little…sad.'

'Not sad, no. Pensive, maybe.'

'What about?'

He laughed and looked away. 'Oh, lots of little things. Nothing you need to worry about.'

But she did. This need for privacy, this *do not enter* that Sam had about him was what had caused a lot of their problems in the first place. He was *meant* to share his worries with her.

Meant to share his concerns, his fears. She was his *wife*.

'Is it work?'

Sam shrugged. 'I am keen to get back. To me, even though logically I know the centre's open and I've worked there, I don't remember that. I want to walk the halls. I want to meet patients…'

'Of course. I have to keep reminding myself of that fact. That you don't remember. You don't know. That what's normal to me is still the unknown to you. I mean… I've *seen* you there at the Monterey. I've watched you work.'

For a while there was silence except for the sound of the boat moving through the water, the splash and the creak of the oars in their housing either side of the boat. The water had a pleasant aroma to it—of fresh and vibrant greenery, of summer, of *life*.

Emily laid a hand upon her belly, thinking of her child's future. 'Sometimes I can't quite believe the way things have turned out myself.'

She saw him glance at her belly, and then he turned to negotiate their arrival at the island beneath the temple. He got up and jumped out, using the chain from the boat to moor them to the wooden pier. Then he reached out his hand and helped her off the boat, before going back to retrieve the picnic basket.

They headed up the steps to the temple.

The round temple was beautiful in its simplicity, with a domed roof and gorgeous views out across the lake. The setting sun reflected light off the surface, glinting as if the water was filled with jewels, and they stood appreciating it for just a moment.

Sam gazed down at his wife and noticed that her hand was still laid across her gently swelling abdomen.

He loved her so much. Was he going to ruin everything with his doubts? Would she see him for the fraud that he was? But then maybe—perhaps—he wasn't the only one with doubts? Emily had never been a mother before. Perhaps she was scared, too?

'Does the future worry you, Em?'

She gazed over the beautiful lake. 'A bit. Becoming a parent is new territory for both of us.'

He nodded. 'It is.'

'Even though I wanted this baby, I know you didn't. But it happened anyway. I always thought it would be something we would want together. That we would make it happen together.'

'We did. Despite our arguments, it seems.'

'We were drunk.'

He let out a sigh. 'Lots of babies are conceived from a drunken night.'

'I worry about whether I'll be a good mother. It's not like I was given the best example of how to do it.'

Sam frowned. He couldn't remember much about her family situation. Had she told him before? He couldn't recall.

'Tell me.'

She looked back at Sam. *Yes.* These were the things they needed to talk about. But she couldn't imagine it would be a comfortable conversation, standing here like this. This was going to be a conversation that would take time.

'Let's see if there's a blanket in that picnic basket, because this stone step is uncomfortable.'

They opened it up and, sure enough, attached to the lid of the basket was a folded, padded blanket, which they laid upon the ground. Once they were settled, and Sam had poured each of them some sparkling water, Emily continued with her story.

'You remember I don't really have any close family?'

He nodded. 'Just your aunt and uncle.'

'That's right.'

'Have you told me much about them? In the last two years, I mean?'

'I've told you the bare bones, but never the full story.'

'So tell me now.' He laid his hand on hers.

She appreciated his support and comfort. Appreciated that he was ready to listen. Open to strengthening their bonds. It was why she'd wanted to bring him to this place. What they both needed to do if they were going to move forward together. And if she shared first then maybe Sam would do so afterwards.

'My mother had always been a rebellious woman, from what Aunt Sylvia told me. If there were conventions and rules and expectations to break, then my mother did that. She got pregnant with me, without being married—which, as my aunt was fond of telling me, caused a great scandal, as if it had happened in Victorian times.

The fact that my mother never knew who my father was made it worse. Apparently there were many candidates.'

Sam rubbed her hand in sympathy.

'Anyway, my mother looked after me for about six months after I was born. I don't remember her, or that time. I was too young. I do have a photograph of me on her knee. My mother was into music, big-time, and she absolutely adored this one particular band. When they came into town to play she went to see them, was invited to an after-show party and that was that. She fell madly in love and simply *had* to be with this man, *had* to travel with him when they went on tour. Only a baby didn't fit into her plans, so she turned up at my Aunt Sylvia's house one day and asked if she would look after me for the night.'

'For one night?'

Emily nodded. 'Only she lied. She never came back and I got left behind. Forgotten about.'

'I'm sure she didn't forget you.'

'I never heard from her again. I can't have been a concern to her.'

'I'm sorry.'

'Sylvia and Martin were not best pleased—no

one would be, to be honest. You agree to baby-sit, grudgingly, for the child of a sister you never really got on with and she never comes back… They were furious. My aunt and uncle did their best, but they weren't natural parents. I was a demanding baby, just starting to learn to sit up and grab things and squeal. They had nothing for me, apart from what my mother had left, and they suddenly had to find money to buy nappies, extra food, clothing, toys… Uncle Martin didn't have the best of health either. He suffered from a really bad back. And suddenly he had to work all these extra shifts, plus overtime, to help pay for me. I hardly saw him.'

'And your aunt?'

'She'd never wanted children. Not really. She'd grown up with my mother, who had apparently stolen all the attention of their parents. My mother was "the pretty one", the "clever one". Although Sylvia never said as much, I kind of got the feeling that she felt second-best. Never appreciated as much. Never loved as much. And now here she was, having to look after her sister's child.

'They tried to make me happy, but I could

feel the resentment from them both. They never said anything outright, but…it wasn't right. So as a child I dreamt of happy, loving families, all sitting around a dinner table, laughing and joking and enjoying being with each other. I pictured what it would be like if we were happy. What our family portraits might look like. But we never did anything like that. There were photos, of course. Plenty of them. Just not the kind I wanted.'

'Your aunt and uncle sound like they struggled a bit.'

'They did their best. But my aunt never really got over her resentment of my mother, who seemed to have freedom and the world at her feet while they took care of her mistake.'

'Is that how you see yourself? As a mistake?'

'How could I not? I wanted to be loved so much. I wanted them to put their arms around me and give me a proper cuddle. I wanted someone to tell me that they loved me and that I was their whole world.'

'*I* did.'

She smiled, feeling tears at the backs of her eyes. 'Yes, you did. Meeting you was the best thing in my life—after my work. The first time we met at the hospital there was something about you that made me feel as if I couldn't even breathe.'

'How did you become a midwife? What made you go down that path? Was it something Sylvia suggested?'

'No. I saw a documentary on television. Sylvia and Martin were out at a church dinner with friends, and there was a documentary on following the journey of an embryo from single cell to living baby. It was all so fascinating to me, and when they showed the birth… The miracle of the baby being born was one thing, but all I could see was the look in the eyes of the mom and dad. Such joy…such love. Pure elation. I wanted to experience that.'

'So you started training?'

She nodded. 'I worked hard at school and got to college. So I could experience that love again and again and again. I think a small part of me wanted to believe that was how my mother had felt when she had me. It's a privilege to be in the room when a mom gives birth. I didn't realise how special it would make me feel. How honoured. I loved it. I still do. But I've always craved experiencing it myself.'

Sam let out a big sigh. 'You had it tough. With your aunt and uncle, I mean.'

'Some people have it tougher.'

Sam sipped his drink.

'What about you, Sam?'

'What do you mean?'

'Tell me more about your family. I don't really know much about them, apart from their names and what they do for a living. We hardly see them. I think the most I ever saw them was at the wedding, and then they kept themselves to themselves.'

Sam let out a big sigh. 'Where do I start?'

'At the beginning.'

He gazed at her and nodded with some reluctance. 'There really isn't much to tell.'

'I think there is. Please, Sam. I feel apart from you. I feel like I'm stuck on this tiny island and you're far out to sea with a rescue boat but you won't come in to land. We need to talk…we need to share who we are so that we can start afresh. Unburdened. Nothing hidden.' She laid a hand on his. 'I know you have a secret, Sam. I don't know what it is, but I want you to feel you can share it with me. If you don't we'll always be apart. We won't get to fix *this*.' She brushed his wedding ring.

Sam's fingers enveloped hers and his thumb stroked the back of her hand. 'I don't want to lose you, Em.'

'I don't want to lose you either. Whatever it is, you can tell me. I won't judge. I won't say anything. I'll just listen.'

He exhaled. A big, heavy sigh. 'It's hard for me.'

'I know. These things usually are. But I know from experience that they always seem massive until you unburden yourself, and then you feel a little better. A little lighter. You know what they say. A problem shared…'

'Is a problem halved?'

She smiled. 'I love you, Sam. I'm your *wife*. You need to be able to tell me.'

'I've never shared it with anyone. None of us have.'

'None of you? Your family?'

Okay, this is a start.

He nodded.

'Then maybe it's time?'

She hoped he would tell her. Whatever it was, if he and his family had kept this burden under wraps for so long then it was time it was given some air. It was like carrying a weight. No matter how small the weight, the longer you had to carry it the heavier it got—until you collapsed from under it.

'You're sure I've never told you anything?'

'I'm sure. Come on—tell me. I want to know you properly, Sam Saint, and we've only ever skimmed the surface of who you are. I've spilled my family secrets. What are yours?'

She'd told him about everything. Her runaway mother. Feeling like she was a mistake. Being left behind. Abandoned. Emily didn't want their child to feel it was a mistake, too. Conceived on a drunken night, during a truce between its parents, and then abandoned by its father. Not loved enough. Worthless.

She wouldn't accept that. She wasn't just fighting for her marriage here, but for her child. *Their* child.

She saw the agony on his face. The internal wrangling going on inside his head. The anguish. She knew his instincts were to keep it hidden still. It was what he had always done. But her words had clearly had an effect on him and she could tell that he knew what she said was true. If they didn't tell each other everything then their relationship would be doomed to fail. Already so much of who he was, was hidden by the amnesia. He didn't need to hide even more.

'You know I have five siblings and Mom and Dad…?'

She smiled and squeezed his fingers in encouragement, her heart beating faster. *He was going to share.* 'I do…'

'Well, the thing you may not know is that Dad and I don't really get on.'

'Really? You seemed okay at the wedding.'

It was true. Sam and his family had been nothing but delightful to one another. Sam had seemed incredibly warm to his mother and his younger siblings. To his dad he'd been… She saw the flash of memory. Sam standing stiff and formal, shaking his father's hand but keeping his distance. Not really talking, just a slight inclination of his head. An acknowledgement that his father had at least come to their wedding.

'Was there a free bar at the wedding? That would have kept my dad happy.'

Emily frowned. 'But he's not a drunk, is he?'

'He's a...social drinker. He has his friends that he sees every day down at the bar. I hated it that a lot of our money as a family got poured down Dad's throat when there were so many mouths to feed.'

'You're the oldest, right?'

'Yes. There's two years between me and Daniel, then a year later there was Clara then Warren, then Caleb.' He paused, looking out across the water. 'And then there was Serena.'

Emily blinked. *What?* But Sam was one of *five* siblings. Not six.

'Serena?'

Sam shook his head and got up to begin pacing, uncomfortable with this subject but knowing he had to tell her. They were married! And she was right—she had to hear this. Or they'd be torn apart because the guilt he felt over Serena's death was the one thing that was still tearing *him* apart, making him doubt his abilities to be a father.

'The only good thing my dad did was give me

brothers and sisters—but all I saw growing up was my mother, heavily pregnant again, struggling to get things done. As the oldest, I had to help, and because Dad was never around, always at the bar, I sort of became a father as well as a big brother to them all.'

'That must have been hard for you.'

'Yeah, well… I don't like to focus on upsetting things.'

'I've noticed. You're a driven man. You've always wanted to be successful. Always busy.'

'It's how I was when I was a teen. There was always something to do—mow the lawn, fix a kitchen cabinet, a leaky faucet. You name it, I worked out how to do it. Because my dad couldn't.'

'Because he wasn't there?'

Sam nodded once. 'My dad was out drinking when my mom gave birth to Warren.'

'Home birth?'

'It was the same for all of us. I can remember being incredibly scared when Warren was born. Mom seemed in a lot of pain, but she was really cool about it in between contractions, you know? Like it was the most normal thing—which it was. But I was only eight. I didn't understand. The midwife asked Mom if she wanted me in the room for the birth and she said it was up to me.'

'And you said yes?'

'No. I was too scared. All the noise Mom was making was…incredible. I'd never heard anything like it. And that was *my mom*, you know? I can remember cowering in my bedroom, listening to her in the next room, wondering why my dad wasn't there to help her. It seemed to go on for hours—it probably actually did—and then there was this second of silence before I heard a new sound. A baby. Crying. And then there was laughter and joy and I could hear my mother crying again, but this time for another reason. I went back in and there she was, propped up in bed, smiling, tears of joy running down her face… It was the most amazing thing I ever saw.'

Emily smiled.

'I remember telling my schoolfriends all about it. They all thought it was weird!' He smiled at the memory. 'And then Mom told us all she was expecting again. I couldn't wait.'

'An OB/GYN in the making?'

He laughed ruefully. 'I guess. I was eleven

when Caleb was born, and yet again I got to hear this miracle from the next room. I started telling anyone who would listen that I wanted to be a doctor when I grew up, so that I could deliver babies every day and witness the joy.'

She loved the enthusiasm in his voice at the memory of his happiness. She was elated that he still had all his past memories. They were important. He might have lost all sense of who he was and *that* would have been terrible.

'And Serena?' she asked with concern.

'I was sixteen years old when Serena was born. My mom swore this was her last baby, and once again I got to hear my baby sister come into the world. She was tiny. Only six pounds. But she was beautiful. She didn't cry. She seemed quite content and calm. That was how my mom named her. Because she was so serene. That was all she kept saying. *"She's so serene."* The midwife suggested it as a name.'

'It's beautiful.'

'Things were tough. Six mouths to feed, plus their own—my parents were struggling hard. Mom would clean other people's houses for extra money, taking the little ones with her in a playpen. I already had a paper round and gave my parents most of my wages to help out. But all our money seemed to go over the bar, and I hated my dad for doing that. My mom struggled to put food on the table every day, but she did it. She made sure we were happy. And then one day I thought to myself, *Who's making Mom happy?* Dad wasn't. She wasn't. She didn't have time. So I took on extra rounds. The second I finished school I'd be out on my bike, hauling papers across yards, all around the neighbourhood. I saved the money. Kept it. When Serena was about four months old I suggested to my dad that he ought to take Mom out for a meal. Nothing expensive. Just a burger or something. I felt Mom needed it, you know?'

Emily nodded.

'I said I'd babysit.' Sam gazed out across the water and watched as a swan glided across its surface, followed by another about a metre behind. 'My mom had never left us before. She didn't want to go. I made her do it. Said she deserved a night out.'

'You wanted her to have a break?'

'Yeah. I had some tests to revise for, so I fed

the kids, made sure they had their baths, and after Serena had had her bottle of milk I changed her nappy and put her in her room for the night.'

Emily could tell the bad part was coming. Sam looked pained, with lines across his brow, and his narrowed eyes were stuck somewhere in the past. He kept rubbing at his forehead, as if the telling of the story was causing him physical pain.

'I checked on them all after an hour. They were asleep. They'd always been good sleepers. Never played up. They were all good kids.'

'What happened?'

'I thought they were okay. I made popcorn and sat down to watch a movie on the television. Mom and Dad came home and Mom, being anxious, went to check on them all.'

Emily laid a hand upon his arm to still him.

'Mom *screamed*. I can still hear it so clearly up here.' He tapped the side of his skull. 'Bloodcurdling, it was. Like someone had wrenched her heart from her chest. Something *had*.'

'Serena.'

'They said it was Sudden Infant Death Syndrome. Nothing anyone could have done. Nothing anyone could have predicted. She just…died. The paramedics tried to revive her when they got to the house. I can remember sitting in the front room, hiding in the corner, hugging my legs and rocking, seeing the red-blue lights flickering through the windows and hearing footsteps above me. And all the time my mother crying. Wailing. Begging for it not to be so…'

'Sam, I'm so sorry.'

She pulled him into her arms and held him as tightly as she could. No wonder he had never told her this story. It was awful! Terrible! She couldn't imagine that happening. Not in her worst nightmares could she conceive how you would get through something like that. She knew that people *did*. They had clients at the Monterey who had lost children before, and she'd always been awed by their bravery and outlook on life.

Was this why Sam had never wanted children? Was this why they'd had so many arguments? He'd never told her before and now she could see why. And yet she'd pushed him, asking him over and over, until in the end she'd just given up and they'd stopped talking.

She felt so bad! Of course she'd wondered *why*

he refused to talk to her about this, but now she knew. And she felt terrible for having pushed so hard.

'I should never have forced my parents to go out. I should have paid more attention to Serena. I should have checked on her more often. I failed her. I was meant to be looking after her and she died and—'

'Sam you were sixteen years old! You were still a child yourself. You can't shoulder that burden. They told you it was an accident. Sudden. It wasn't your fault.'

'It feels that way.'

'Is that why you never want to see your family? Why you never want them to visit?'

'I see it in their faces when they look at me. Like an unspoken accusation.'

She shook her head and grabbed his arms, making him look at her. 'They probably just miss you! Their big brother who always looked out for them suddenly doesn't want them around. They're probably hurt. They look up to you, Sam. Even I could see that. It's possible they're just wondering what they did wrong.'

He looked down at his wife's face. 'They did nothing wrong. It was me.'

'It was *not you.* You were babysitting. You did everything right. You bathed her, fed her, changed her nappy, put her to bed. That's what millions of parents do every night. They don't stand over their children's cots and count every breath. It's impossible.'

He still looked shame-faced. Still looked guilty. But he'd made a start in sharing his burden. She was glad that he had told her. And suddenly she realised. Suddenly she remembered.

'The candle was for Serena.'

He met her gaze. 'Yes.'

She let out a long, slow, steadying breath. 'Thank you for telling me, Sam. Now I understand why you—' She stopped before she could blurt out any more. He didn't need to hear that. They were here to *heal*. Paris was healing their hearts as well as their minds.

'I'm afraid, Em. Afraid that I won't be able to protect *our* baby.' He laid a hand on her belly, gently stroking it, then knelt down in front of her, laying his head against her belly as if trying to hear a heartbeat. 'What if I fail our child?'

Her heart was almost torn in two as she heard the heartbreak in his voice. He'd agonised over this. 'You won't. It's okay to be afraid, Sam. It's okay to have fears. All parents do.'

He lifted his head to look at her. 'Do *you*?' He seemed to doubt her words.

Emily rushed to reassure him. 'Of course I do! What do I know about being a great mother? Did I have a fabulous role model? Did my aunt provide me with a loving example? No. Neither of them did. I worry that I'll get this wrong all the time. What if I'm awful at being a mom? At something that I've wanted for *so long*?'

'You'll be perfect.'

'And so will you. Believe me, Sam, I know you will. You care so much. But you know what? We can be afraid together and struggle together. We're strong that way. We're determined. Driven. Remember?'

Sam stood and looked down into her face. 'What would I do without you, Mrs Saint?'

'Let's hope you never have to find out.' She smiled. 'Look, we're here—in the Temple of Love. Let's make a promise to each other to always be open and share our fears. If there's a problem, we tell each other about it. Deal?'

'Deal.'

Sam pulled her towards him for a kiss. It felt like the start of something new. An opening. An honesty between them that had never been there before. Her lips on his sealed the promise that their hearts were making.

'Thank you for telling me, Sam. It means so much to me.'

'You're right. I do feel different for having said it out loud.'

'The pain won't go. Not totally. But it can be different now—just you see.'

'Thanks, Em.'

He pulled her close once more and they stood there, in the Temple of Love, enveloped in each other's arms, and just held each other.

Em knew they'd taken a huge step forward today. She'd been right to bring him here. To ask him to share this. It shed new light on all Sam's past behaviour. Perhaps she had enlightened him, too, on why having a baby had meant so much to her?

There was still so much for them to do, but

right now things were moving in a positive direction.

She could only foresee it getting better.

CHAPTER SEVEN

THEY HAD A beautiful evening picnic. The hotel had packed some delightful food in the basket—a *salade niçoise* with mixed herbs, olives, anchovies and potatoes, a sausage and potato *galette,* a *haricots verts* salad with quail eggs and tiny shrimp, goat's cheese and tomatoes. There was also raspberry *clafoutis,* pound cake and *sables* biscuits, all served with a small bottle of white wine, sparkling and still water, and a tiny bottle of alcohol-free rhubarb wine.

They sat in the temple, overlooking the water, quietly eating their evening meal and enjoying the sounds of nature in the air: the occasional duck quacking, the lapping of the water below, the wind rustling the trees.

Eventually Sam packed everything back into the basket, and on their way down the rocky stairway to the boat they paused a moment to look inside the grotto. The stony caves were a mix of dark and light, jagged rocks and stalactites.

'This place is like us, really,' Sam observed.

Emily turned to him. 'How do you mean?'

'Well, there's the beautiful Temple of Love on show for everyone to see, and it all looks wonderful. But then you dig deeper, you come down here, and there's a dark place—forbidding and scary.'

Emily stepped out of the caves' darkness, through one of the openings, to move out towards the lessening light of the day.

'But, using your analogy, we've come through it together this time and we both know it's there.'

He nodded. 'True.'

Sam still wasn't sure that he should have told Emily everything. The uselessness of his own father… Serena's brief yet painful story. He wasn't used to sharing things like that. He'd never done it and it felt strange. It made him feel naked. Exposed when he'd always had a protective wall around him.

He knew the story was safe with Emily, but did she really grasp how much his past affected him?

He'd not had a great father figure. In his eyes

his father had been good for two things—making babies and drinking beer. Sam had been a better father to those kids than his own dad had—but on the other hand he had also let them down. He'd devastated them. It had been *his* plan to send his parents out for the night. *His* plan to make his mother go out. When he'd checked on Serena that time and assumed she was sleeping because she was so still, so quiet, had she really been sleeping? Or had she already passed away?

It haunted him—the idea that he might have looked down upon his baby sister with love, not realising that she lay there dead.

I should have known.

The guilt still tore him apart, and the pain was still incredibly strong. And he still felt to blame. But Emily had welcomed the load. Had asked to take it on, no matter what it was. Had said that, as his wife, she was there to help him carry it. Make it easier.

But he doubted it would ever be that. Easier.

The plain fact of the matter now was, though, that Emily knew. Perhaps from here they could have a conversation about his fears about becoming a parent. About caring for this baby to come. His son or daughter.

They would need a strong marriage. Raising a child was not easy. He knew how difficult it could be. Okay, so he and Emily did not have the financial worries his own parents had had, but it was still hard. And they would need to be united. He knew from the flashes of memory he'd had, and the admissions Em had made, that their marriage had deteriorated—and quickly.

That concerned him greatly.

He loved this woman so much, and yet they had both allowed it to crumble so quickly because neither of them had been able to talk the way they had today.

Perhaps it took nearly losing your life, being in a terrible accident, having amnesia, to turn it around? To admit the problems and vow to work through them?

He reached out to place his hand in the small of her back and guided her safely down the steps towards the boat. She turned to look at him, flashed him a smile, and—

They were walking down the aisle. Newly married. Sun gleamed through the church win-

dows and everyone was smiling. He looked up and saw his mother's face. She was crying with happiness, her hands clutched together before her chest as if in prayer, and she was mouthing something to him. He couldn't catch her words, and then as he passed her she reached out and took his hand.

'Live, Sam. Be happy now.'

He'd smiled back. Nodded. Promised that he would. And then he'd turned back to his wife and she'd looked at him and smiled and...

He helped Emily into the boat. Made sure she was seated safely before he put the picnic basket inside and unchained the boat from the pier. With one of the wooden oars he pushed them away from the small island, and they drifted out across the water and he began to row.

His mother had wanted him to be happy. *Be happy now.* Had his own mother seen how unhappy he'd been at home after Serena died? He'd tried to make up for it. He'd tried his best to prove that he was still a good son afterwards. But nothing had made his mother smile after that.

But she smiled at the wedding. She was happy for me. She didn't resent my happiness.

Perhaps he ought to take the time actually to try and enjoy life. Was this why he was so driven? Filling his days with work and other distractions just so that he wasn't thinking about Serena? Was that why his marriage had begun to fail? Instead of looking at the faults they had created, the problems they shared, he'd done what he'd always done—pushed it to one side and filled up his time with work.

He'd thought that by ignoring the issues they would go away.

The revelation was startling.

He stopped rowing and the boat drifted quietly across the water.

Night had settled across Paris when they returned to their hotel. Emily donned the beautiful new powder-blue dress that Sam had secretly bought for her and stood in front of the mirror admiring it.

Sam came up behind her and slid his hands over her burgeoning abdomen. It was still only a slight swelling, but she smiled, looking at the reflection of his face in the mirror.

He looked content. And that was something she hadn't seen for such a long time.

'The dress is beautiful, Sam. Thank you.'

'You're more beautiful.'

Her cheeks bloomed in the mirror and she laid her hands upon his, their fingers entwining. She looked up at him, hesitant.

Was it too soon? Was it just right? If she pushed for them to make love now would it be wrong? Or just perfect?

She felt so much closer to Sam now. Before she'd described him as being on a rescue boat far out to sea, miles away from her, but since his confession—since he'd told her about his family and about Serena especially—she'd felt as if he was within arms' reach.

Should she test it and see?

She missed him. She missed the intimacy that they'd once shared. Surely now there was nothing that could keep them apart? Being together physically, emotionally, mentally, surely would just strengthen the bond that they were both trying to enforce?

She met his gaze in the reflection. 'Undo the zip.'

He looked into her eyes. 'You've just put it on.'

'Yes. And now I want you to take it off me.'

He looked hesitant. And for a brief moment she thought she'd pushed him too soon. Had asked, once again, for too much. But then—wonderfully—she watched in the mirror as his hands slid from hers, went to the zip at the nape of her neck and slowly, delicately, drew it down.

She could feel his heated breath on the back of her neck, and she closed her eyes as she felt him slip the dress from her shoulders, his hands following close after, trailing over her shoulders, arms, her hips.

The beautiful dress dropped to the floor and Emily turned to face him.

'I love you, Sam, and I want you to love me.'

'I do.' His voice was deep, emotional.

'Show me.'

Sam stared deeply into her eyes for a brief, yet agonising moment, before he finally took her in his arms and kissed her.

Emily sank into his embrace.

This was what she had craved! It had never been about the great sex, the making love. It had been about the deep intimacy they had shared when they had been together physically. The closeness, the connection. The unity.

Before, when they had been together, it had been great. Sam was a brilliant lover. But because she had never truly known her husband, never known all his secrets, there had never been that level of *trust* and *vulnerability* between them. Emily had always felt somehow, that she was being kept in the dark, and it had made her wonder if he had truly loved her.

But now she felt she *knew* him. Knew his fears. His pain. His hurt. She knew his vulnerabilities, as he did hers, and now they were equal.

She closed her eyes and gave herself up to Sam. *This* was what they needed to do. Be close like this. Intimate. They were working towards a greater good within their marriage and this was what both of them needed right now. To solidify that bond…to unite them in their vows.

As his hands and lips moved deftly over her body Emily found herself losing her train of thought. His lips upon her collarbone, her neck, were delightful. His hands had easily unclipped her bra and were now beautifully paying attention to her sensitive breasts, making her gasp and close her eyes…

Her hands were on his body…*too many clothes...*

He helped her remove them and once again she marvelled at his powerful, muscular body. The broad expanse of him, the wide shoulders, the narrow waist, the long, lean legs, his erection pressing against her stomach…

Sam scooped her up and placed her on the bed with a gentleness that belied his size. His thumbs hooked into her underwear and she lifted her bottom so that he could remove it, and then he covered her with his body as his lips began to explore even more.

Right now she just wanted to enjoy. Sam's lips. Sam's tongue. Sam's body. Moving over…*into* her.

Emily gasped, arching her body up against him as he drove in deep.

Afterwards, sated, they lay together in bed, Sam behind his wife.

It had felt good to be with her. It had felt *right*. This was where he was supposed to be. This was who he was supposed to be with. He knew it in his bones and he was feeling much better now about having shared.

It had brought them closer. Which was odd. That something so painful, so hurtful, had been the gateway for the two of them to connect.

Life was strange that way.

All this time he had kept it from her and in turn it had kept them apart. Obviously the old Sam hadn't been able to see that. Or maybe he had, but hadn't known what to do about it. How must it have felt to have seen his marriage crumbling?

He shuddered inside, glad his memories about that had not come back fully. He wasn't sure he wanted them—not now. Not now that things had changed. Now they were ready to face their future together. As one.

There was still fear about his ability as a father, but it seemed…less. How was that? All he'd done was voice it. Something he'd always believed would be the worst thing ever. He had feared that Emily would be appalled. How had he allowed himself to believe that?

But he guessed he had learned it from his parents. No one at home spoke about Serena ever. Mom was permanently depressed. Dad stayed away.

I stayed away! Was I being like my own father? A man I'd always hated for staying away and not being there?

Sam closed his eyes at the thought and pressed his lips to Emily's shoulder.

'You know, Sam, I've been thinking, and there are things that we can do.'

He frowned. 'What about?'

'When the baby arrives. Keeping it safe.'

She was so sweet. Thinking of his concerns. Knowing what he must be feeling.

'Oh?'

'We could get a monitor. Not just one of those walkie-talkie-type things, but one of those oxygen monitors—like a SATs device. We'd be able to keep an eye on it as the baby sleeps. We'd make sure it's in the *feet to foot* position in the cot, make sure no blankets cover it's head by getting a sleepsuit instead—things like that.'

He pressed the length of his body against hers. 'Thank you.'

'What for?'

'For trying to ease my worries.'

She half turned and reached for him. 'How could I not? You've already been through too much loss.'

'My whole family has.'

'I think you and your family ought to talk to someone. A counsellor, perhaps. Do you think they'd be open to that?'

'I don't know. All they've ever done is block it out.'

'And look what that did. I nearly lost you, Sam—we let it come between us. It was my fault, too. I kept pushing when I should have stopped to ask myself why.'

'You couldn't have known.'

'I could have if we'd been closer. If instead of just accepting what life had dealt us we'd fought against it. We both brought bad habits into our marriage and let them rule us, never pausing for a moment to think if it was right.'

'We worked it out in the end.'

'Yes, we did.' She smiled.

'Paris did the trick.'

'It always does.'

And as he moved to kiss her, and to make love

to her once again, Emily pushed the thought of telling Sam the whole truth away.

Paris *had* helped—but not in the way they'd ever thought or hoped. They had found each other in another way, and it was better than anything she'd ever hoped for.

There was still time for Sam's memories to come back, too, and if they did she felt sure they'd be okay.

They were strong again.

They were close.

They were united.

CHAPTER EIGHT

THEY COULD NOT come to Paris without exploring the Eiffel Tower. They had deliberately left it till last, despite the way it overlooked them, like a guardian, whilst they slept in their hotel room.

'So, we have a choice. Do we want to climb the steps or use the lifts to reach each level?'

Em laughed. 'Considering my condition, I'm not sure I want to climb three hundred steps.'

'The lift it is.'

They stood at the base, craning their necks backwards to look up to the top.

It was an incredibly powerful sight. Only when you were close could you really understand its size and the work that had gone into its construction.

Emily took some photographs of them both, determined to get some pictures of them together into her phone. And then they were in the lift, travelling up with about eight others.

Opposite them was a woman, heavily pregnant, with her sprawling abdomen spilling over the top of her trousers. Emily smiled at her, imagining herself at that size in a few months. It wouldn't take long. And she couldn't wait to feel the baby kick and move around.

The woman was rubbing her hand over her abdomen.

'How many weeks are you?' asked Emily, hoping the woman spoke English.

She did. 'Thirty-five. This is our last trip before our world descends into chaos!' The woman laughed good-naturedly.

'You're British?'

'Yes. We came through the Channel Tunnel. I'm not allowed to fly now. You're American?'

Emily nodded. 'Second honeymoon.'

'Oh. Congratulations.'

'To you, too.'

The lift slowed to a stop and the doors opened. They got out on the first level of the tower.

Paris lay spread out beneath them and it looked so different. The rooftops, the buildings old and new, all basking in the afternoon sunshine.

'Look at that, Sam!'

'I see it.'

They both breathed in the view. There was something very calm and relaxing about looking at the city from here. Traffic bustled below, but up here there was a sense of peace. Of reflection.

Emily glanced around her and saw the woman from the lift. She was rubbing at the small of her back and looked uncomfortable. She nodded to Sam. 'Think she's okay?'

'I'm sure it's just backache. You'll get that big one day, and know exactly how she feels.'

Emily smiled. 'Remind me to enjoy it. I imagine I'll be quite nervous by the time I'm at thirty-five weeks.'

He draped his arm around her shoulders. 'I promise you I'll rub your feet.'

'Will you shave my legs for me?'

Sam smiled. 'I'll even paint your toenails.'

'Ooh. Can't wait, then!'

They took in the story window, showing the construction of the Eiffel Tower, and read about how the old hydraulic lifts had worked.

'Architects are amazing, when you think about it.'

'*You're* an architect, don't forget. You're building our baby. Think of all the work that goes into *that*!'

'Hmm, no wonder I get tired.' She ran her hand over her stomach. 'Should we go up to the second floor?'

Sam nodded, and back into the lift they got.

On the second floor they viewed the panoramic maps and a small red scale model of the original top of the Eiffel Tower from 1889. There was even a champagne bar.

'Hmm, not for me, though…' Emily mused.

'No. Got to look after the little one.'

She smiled at him and reached out to hold his hand. This was nice. Being able to talk about the baby easily to each other. Before it had always seemed a taboo subject. One that she shouldn't raise, knowing Sam's objections. But it was different now. And she could see them getting close to that ideal family picture she had of an excited couple preparing to welcome their new baby into the world. It was thrilling.

They got into the glass lift and ascended to the top. It was spectacular up there, but the wind riffled through her hair so much Emily had to keep tucking it behind her ears.

They were able to view Gustav Eiffel's office, which had been restored to its original layout, with wax models of the man himself and Thomas Edison, but they quickly headed back out to admire Paris.

It needed admiring. It was a truly magical place, and it had worked its magic on their relationship.

Emily felt grateful to it—so much so that her eyes began to water and she thought she might cry. Surreptitiously she wiped her eyes and hoped Sam hadn't noticed.

Once they'd had a good look, and taken some more photographs, they decided to head back down to ground level. It felt a little sad to come back down to earth.

Emily had learnt so much this trip. Not just about Sam, but also about herself, and she'd set herself some new vows—never to let anyone push her away. And if they did to find out why. To see if there was something she could do to put things right.

People, relationships—they were important. Vital. What were any of them without those they loved? Alone. Lonely. Sad. That wasn't a life for anyone, and life was much too short to lose most of it in secrets or regret.

Sam had booked them into a restaurant for their evening meal.

It was a beautiful place. A large *conservatoire*, painted white and lit with lanterns. The wrought-iron furniture was softened by beautifully furnished cushions in bright colours, all complementing each other. Each table was adorned with a glass fishbowl, half filled with water, and in the water floated gerberas and daisies.

Emily took a seat and smiled at Sam. This was their last night in Paris. Soon they would be returning home. Back to reality. To work. The Monterey. Part of her didn't want to go back. She liked it here. She and Sam were in this nice little bubble and everything was right in their world. What if going back home changed everything?

As she pondered this she noticed the heavily pregnant woman from the Eiffel Tower entering the restaurant with her husband. They sat down at a table on the far left. Emily nodded and smiled when the woman looked up.

'I guess we've both got to return to reality when we go back,' she said.

Sam turned to see who she was looking at and nodded hello to the couple, too. 'We'll be okay.'

'I want us to be more than okay, Sam.'

'We will be.' He reached for her hand and squeezed it.

The waiter arrived and presented them with menus, and filled their glasses with water before disappearing.

Emily hid behind her menu for a moment, and then she looked over the top. 'What if we're not?' Her voice trembled on the last word and suddenly she was fighting back tears.

Claiming Sam had meant so much to her! It was her entire life. She loved him, worked with him, was married to him, was carrying his child. What if it all went wrong? She needed him to reassure her.

'Emily...' He put down his menu and leaned forward. 'I know it's scary, but we'll be all right. It's different this time. We won't return home the same people. We can't. We know the dangers now, and what to look out for. We're both fighting for this and I'm not going to let us lose what we have.'

'The Monterey takes up so much of your time, though, Sam. I'm worried it will suck you back in. You haven't seen it in operation yet—what if you're so eager to reacquaint yourself with everything that's going on that I lose you to it? It was our dream to start it, but now—'

'But now it's already up and running. It's successful. And as the boss and CEO I can delegate, right?'

She nodded.

'Time for us, as a couple, will take priority.'

'Okay.' Slightly reassured, she looked back down at the menu.

Everything sounded delicious, and she felt hungry enough to want to try it all. In the end she chose a French onion soup to start, a fennel and lavender lamb *noisette* for main and a *croquembouche* for dessert.

Sam ordered the same, not wanting to try the seafood, thinking it might make her feel ill.

Above them twinkling stars could be seen through the glass, and the French doors of the *conservatoire* opened up to a beautiful rose garden with a small fountain at its centre.

'It's beautiful here. I really don't think I'm ever going to forget Paris.'

'Nor me.' Sam smiled. 'Not this time.'

'Have you had any more flashbacks? Anything?'

'Not for a while.'

'It doesn't mean they've stopped.'

'I know. I'm not worried. They'll come back.' He took a sip of his water. 'You know what was great, though?'

'What?'

'For the first time today I actually pictured myself becoming a father. Wanting to be one. Holding our child in my arms. Looking down into its face.' He seemed wistful. 'I remember holding each of my siblings just after they were born, and how that felt, but to hold your *own child* must feel...incredible!'

'Oh, Sam, I'm so pleased.' She smiled back, knowing how much he'd feared becoming a father. To be thinking about it, imagining it in positive terms, was a huge leap forward for him. 'Is it scary still?'

'A bit. I was always so busy pushing the idea away, telling myself I could never be a father, that it never occurred to me to think about how much I might actually want to be one.'

'You do?'

'I do!' He laughed, incredulous. 'I'm sure you can imagine how surprised I am.'

Emily laughed with him, then sat back as their onion soup arrived, topped with herby croutons and a swirl of cream. The aroma of the onion and the richness of the soup tantalised her senses and she salivated in anticipation. 'Oh, that smells delicious!'

It was. The soup was perfect—not too thin, not too thick, rich with onion and vegetable stock. And the croutons were bite-sized crispy delights.

'It's strange. We came here to Paris to try and get my memories back, but instead I got a completely different gift.'

She smiled, pleased for him—for *them*. The last year of their marriage had been difficult, and she'd lost count of the amount of times she'd wanted Sam to want a child as much as she had. But now, since their talk on the island, they'd become closer, united, and Sam finally felt able to acknowledge that, despite his fears, he did actually want to become a father. It was more than music to her ears—it was a whole orchestra!

Everything was working out for them. And he was right. Paris had surprised them in such different ways from the ones they had expected.

Their lamb dish arrived, steaming and succulent, and the meat just melted in their mouths.

'You're going to make a great father, Sam.'

He smiled back at her with thanks. 'I hope so.'

'I know so. You care so much about getting it right. About being there for your child. How could you be anything else?'

'Well, I appreciate your vote of confidence. You're going to make the most amazing mom, too.'

She hoped so. Becoming pregnant had made her think of so many things. Her own childhood, her marriage, what she wanted for her child… Above all she wanted her child to know without a shadow of a doubt that it was loved by both parents and that it would grow up in a stable family. Her feelings for her baby were already incredibly strong, and she couldn't imagine giving birth to a child and abandoning it six months later. Had her mother ever truly wanted her? Had there ever been that mother-baby bond?

It would be *so* different for their child. She would never make her mother's mistakes.

They were just about to start their *croquembouche*—Emily ready to tuck in with gusto, imagining those cream-filled choux pastry puffs—when there was a loud gasp from the other side of the *conservatoire* and a clanging sound as cutlery hit the floor.

The heavily pregnant woman from the Eiffel Tower had stood up, and was looking down at herself and breathing heavily. 'I think my waters just broke!'

At first Emily felt a surge of excitement for the woman. It might be a bit early, but she was about to meet her child and experience that rush of joy. But then concern filled her as the woman looked at her partner across the table and yelled, *'Something's wrong! I can feel it!'*

Waiters hurried to assist as the other diners all turned to see what was going on. The woman was gasping heavily and trying to feel through her dress.

'Oh, my God, there's something there!'

They could hear the panic in her voice—and rightly so.

Sam and Emily got up from their table and rushed over.

Sam stooped low to make eye contact. 'Remember us? From the tower? My name's Sam and I'm an OB/GYN. Do you want me to take a look?'

The woman looked terrified, and glanced to Emily for reassurance. 'And I'm a midwife. Let us help you.'

But they were in a busy restaurant, and it was almost full. There was no place for a private examination.

Emily looked at a waiter. 'Can you get some tablecloths so we can make a privacy screen?'

The waiter nodded and came back with an armful of cloths and some other members of staff. They all surrounded the frantic woman and raised the tablecloths so that she could be examined without the whole world seeing her so vulnerable.

Sam helped her lower herself to the floor and bundled up a jacket from the back of a chair to go under her head. 'I need to examine you.

I won't touch, but I do need to look. Or would you prefer my wife to do it?'

The woman indicated she would prefer Emily, so they swapped places and Emily lifted the woman's skirt and adjusted her underwear. There was clearly something there that shouldn't be.

Emily turned to Sam. 'She has a prolapsed cord.'

A prolapsed cord was an emergency. The cord was what kept the baby alive, providing it with blood, nutrients and survival. If the baby's head or body compressed the prolapsed cord it might cut off all of that and the result would be foetal hypoxia, brain damage or even death.

If they'd been in a hospital they would have been able to deal with this immediately. They'd have had the equipment. They'd at least have had *gloves*. But here in the *conservatoire* they had nothing.

Sam immediately told the staff to call for an ambulance, and to bring them some hot water to clean their hands.

'What's your name?' he asked the panicking mother.

'C-C-Clare.'

'Okay, Clare, your baby's umbilical cord has prolapsed and we need to prevent compression. I want you to get onto your hands and knees and keep your butt in the air. You need to rest your chest and head against the floor. That's it. Now, my wife will have to press down against the baby, where we can see it. It's very important that she does this in order to ensure the baby is getting what it needs from the umbilical cord. Do you understand?'

Clare was crying. From fear, from embarrassment—he could only guess. But she had to do it if she wanted her baby to survive.

Sam looked at Em. 'Is the cord still pulsing?'

She nodded. It was, which was a good sign. It meant blood and nutrients were still getting to the baby. Now they just needed to keep it that way.

Normally this would never be done without gloves. With the amniotic fluid dispersed, the baby would be open to infection. But they didn't have gloves, so the hot water they'd been brought would have to do.

She found the presenting part of the baby's

head pressing low. She provided pressure and felt the pulse in the cord strengthen. *Good.*

'Okay, it's working.'

Sam nodded. 'You're doing brilliantly, Clare. I know this isn't how you imagined it, but an ambulance is on its way, and before you know it you'll have this baby in your arms. Just keep thinking about that, okay? That's the important part.'

Clare nodded furiously.

They kept talking to her, trying to keep Clare's mind off what was happening to her. They even managed to make her laugh at one point. Just a small laugh. Nervous and timid. But she was looking braver.

Emily kept her eyes on Sam. He was being brilliant, lying down low on the ground, face to face with Clare, keeping her calm, keeping her positive, telling her about all the babies he'd delivered and how he'd met his wife through one such delivery. How pregnancy and birth brought different surprises, and how at the end all that mattered was a safe and healthy baby.

By the time the paramedics arrived Clare was clutching Sam's hand and staring deeply into his eyes as if he was her own personal birthing coach. Clare's husband held his wife's other hand and she was very carefully manoeuvred into the ambulance.

'There is no room for all,' the paramedic said.

'They're all coming!' insisted Clare.

But with Emily still applying pressure, and Clare still clutching Sam's hand, her husband shouted that he'd take his car. His wife's safety was clearly a priority right now.

The journey to the hospital took minutes, and Clare was rushed into the *maternité* suite, given high-flow oxygen, as she had been in the ambulance, and rushed into Theatre for an emergency Caesarean section. Her husband had not yet arrived—obviously unable to keep up with the speeding ambulance in a city he did not know.

'I want George here!' Clare insisted.

Sam shook his head. 'There's no time, Clare. I'm sorry. They've got to operate.'

Emily tried to reassure her patient as they were whisked into Theatre, with Sam left behind to wait for Clare's husband.

Once they were in the operating theatre events

moved at a frightening speed for the woman on the table.

Emily did her best, trying to reassure Clare, and within seconds her baby was being lifted out of Clare's womb. Instantly it began to cry.

Emily, who had been gowned by a theatre assistant, had stepped back once the baby had been safely delivered, and she stood by the far wall as the baby was presented to the new mother. A little girl. As Clare took her new daughter in her arms the doors burst open and a frantic pair of eyes looked out over a mask, widening when they saw his wife and new baby.

Emily quietly slipped away from Theatre and found her husband. She reached for Sam's hand and they stood quietly, pondering the events of the last hour or so.

It didn't take long for their patient to come out of Theatre, and soon enough Clare and her husband George were in a postnatal room, enjoying their new daughter.

Emily and Sam wrote notes on what had happened in the restaurant to present to the hospital staff, and were about to leave when a nurse came to find them.

'Clare would like to see you.'

'Really?' Emily was delighted. She hadn't known whether they ought to say goodbye—whether they ought to intrude on Clare and George's first private moments with their baby. At the Monterey they liked to leave a family to get to know one another as quickly as possible when it was safe to do so. Those first moments together, alone as mum and dad and baby, were precious.

They knocked and went in.

Clare was sat up in bed, looking proud and happy with her baby in her arms, and beside her, his arm around his wife's shoulders, was George.

When Sam and Emily entered the room George stood up and came over to shake Sam's hand and give Emily a hug.

'Thank you so much! For all that you did.'

'It was our pleasure.'

'We were *so* lucky that you were there! If you hadn't been…' George shook his head as he tried to imagine such a terrible thing. 'We don't know what would have happened.'

'But we were and it all worked out—that's what's important. How are you feeling, Clare?'

Clare looked happy and content. Her face was a little pale, but there were two rosy spots on her cheeks from beaming at her new baby daughter. 'Fine. I'm absolutely fine!'

Emily and Sam looked down at the baby. Like all newborns she was squinting against the light in the room, snuffling, and trying to gnaw on one of her curled up hands.

'She looks hungry,' said Emily. 'And a good size for thirty-five weeks.'

'Six pounds one, they said.'

'Wow. She'd have been huge if she'd gone to term.'

They laughed.

'What are you going to call her?'

Clare looked at George and he nodded. 'We did think about calling her Emma, but we'd really like to call her Emily—if you wouldn't mind?'

Em gasped, clutching her hands together. 'Really?'

Clare nodded. 'Do you want to hold her?'

Emily took the baby carefully from her mother's arms and quickly glanced at Sam, who was smiling at her.

She'd delivered and held many babies, but this

one seemed special. Perhaps because it had been such an emergency, happening away from a hospital, and they'd had to improvise with the hot water and the tablecloths and the *terror* that it could go so wrong, so quickly. She and Sam had met over a delivery and now, renewed, they had delivered another.

If that cord had become occluded, what would they have done? Performed a C-section in a restaurant without proper equipment? It would have been almost impossible, and Clare would have lost her baby.

They'd been lucky. All of them.

'She's beautiful, Clare.'

Emily passed the baby into Sam's arms. She felt her heart well up to see him standing there, holding the little girl. One day it would be their child. One day he'd be looking down at his own baby. Tears pricked her eyes and she sniffed and wiped them away as he handed the baby back to her mother.

'We'll leave you now. You need time alone.'

'Will you keep in touch? We'd love to send you a photo of baby Emily when she's older.'

They nodded, and wrote down their contact details.

It was hard to step away. But it was the right thing to do. They had merely assisted this baby to come into the world safely. It was like being back at work in a way. They'd done their part and now it was time to let the parents do theirs.

Sam sighed. 'I miss that rush.'

Emily looked at him and gave him a playful nudge. 'Well, technically you're still signed off from work for a while. You can't go back yet.'

'I know, and I'll stick to it. But it has made me wonder what I'll do when we get back. Presumably you'll be back at work?'

She sighed. 'Yes, I will. Don't forget you still don't have all your memories. You need to heal. Just because you don't have massive scars, or a plaster cast, or staples or stitches, it doesn't mean you're better. Your brain took a battering.'

'I know. But I *feel* good. Perhaps I could look to see which spare room we can make into a nursery? Start making plans?'

She turned to him, a smile on her face. 'Really?'

He nodded. 'Really. It'll be fun, I think.'

Emily laughed and reached for his hand once again. 'You make me so happy, Sam.'

'Good. Can I make you happy one more time in our hotel room? Before we have to start packing for our trip home?'

She looked at him, smiled wickedly and nodded.

They spent a rather pleasant few hours in each other's arms, leaving it until the last possible moment before they had to pack and get to the airport for their flight home.

It felt odd to Emily to be walking back through Charles de Gaulle airport. The last time she'd strode through here, through its concourses, she'd been nervous and excited. Wondering whether Paris would recover Sam's memories or not…whether it would make them or break them…whether they would rekindle their relationship and make it strong again.

Paris had exceeded her expectations. No. That wasn't right. *Sam* had exceeded her expectations. Paris had simply been a place. A setting. It was she and Sam who had done all the work. Both of them initially hiding from their feelings, being the people they had always been, but then slowly, after all their time spent together, they'd revealed their true selves.

They had eaten and danced and rowed a boat. They had biked through the artists' quarter and looked out from the Eiffel Tower. They had re-explored the city as much as they had re-explored themselves, finding places to go they had never been before and finding delight and joy and even peace in quiet, dark places.

They were returning to Beverly Hills with a united front. With their marriage a hundred times stronger than it had ever been.

Her dream had come true.

And it didn't matter now if Sam's memories came back. He'd known they'd been arguing, he'd known it had been bad, and they'd both worked out *why*. Now they had a solution and they were strong again. Sam might feel a little sad if the memories came back. Being confronted with some of the things he'd said. Some of the things *she* had said, all in the heat of the moment. But they would get over them. They would be able to reassure each other that it was all in the past.

She knew him now. All of him. Secrets and all. And she loved him more than she ever had. She was so glad, deep in her heart, that she had stayed to fight for him. Stayed to give them both the chance they deserved.

Had she ever thought she'd be discussing how to decorate a nursery with him? Whether they should have an animal or a space theme? Whether to go for soft neutrals or rich primary colours? Had she ever thought that they would discuss names? Or what type of birth she wanted?

She was so looking forward to seeing Sam become a father. Watching him learn and grow, falling in love with their child and having that happy family that she had always dreamed of.

He'd admitted that he was still scared, but who wouldn't be? She'd be worried if he wasn't. *Everyone* was worried when they had a child. Worried that they'd not be able to look after it properly. Worried that they'd mess up. Worried that it might hurt itself one day.

But that was life. No one could be wrapped in a bubble, no matter how much you might want to protect someone.

They would do their best as parents. That was all they *could* do.

As they sat on the plane, and she read the book she'd brought along in her hand luggage, she laid her hand on her abdomen. Soon she would feel her baby move. Soon she would feel kicks and flips and all those little movements mothers-to-be talked about. She would walk the halls of the Monterey pregnant. She would deliver mothers whilst heavily pregnant herself, and they would ask her if she was frightened or scared?

And she knew that she would smile and rub her belly and feel that everything was right in her world.

Sam glanced at his wife, reading her book on the plane and absently rubbing her belly, and wondered if she was as scared of returning home as he was?

They'd got everything so *right* in Paris, and though he was keen to get back to work and restart their life together on a much better footing he still felt nervous.

He'd told Emily the truth when he'd admitted that he actually quite wanted to be a father. He'd come from a big family. He couldn't imagine it ever being just him and Em, even if he had rebelled at the idea of her getting pregnant. He'd loved having lots of siblings. Someone to play with outside, riding bikes and flying kites and making dens. And then, when it rained, playing indoors—hide and seek, cards, board games. Before Serena he remembered laughter. The way his younger siblings would look up to him for guidance.

He'd *loved* that.

To have his *own child* or even *children* do that would be the most marvellous thing he could think of.

But what if he became like his father again? It had been a revelation to him that he'd been doing the same thing. Staying away from home. Ignoring his wife. Okay, he'd not been out drinking their money away, but he'd been pretty much useless to her from all accounts.

Em must have felt so incredibly alone!

He was incredibly grateful to her, though. Because she had fought for him. Fought for their marriage. Fought for his memories. And she'd not mollycoddled him and lied about how they'd been. She'd told him the truth. Admitted they'd had problems. She'd even been scared to tell him she was pregnant!

That seemed such a long time ago. Stuck in hospital like that. Finding that out. He'd been so frightened.

He still was, really. What had happened to Serena would always haunt him, every single day, only now the pain wasn't as unbearable as it had used to be. He would worry about his own child every night. He knew he would. Perhaps he would have his fair share of sleepless nights. But he knew that every day he woke and found his child smiling up at him from its cot or bed he would feel joy and contentment on a scale he could never have imagined.

Work he would have to delegate, as he'd promised. Yes, he had a business to run. But what was more important? Work? Or his family?

He'd always put family first when he was little. He'd had to. Working to bring in money had taken up so much of his time it was probably why he'd found it so easy to let the Monterey consume him when he'd started having problems with Emily.

But he wouldn't let it do that any more. He wanted to be more hands-on with the births, not sitting in an office staring at a spreadsheet. That wasn't what he'd started the business for.

Sam laid his hand upon his wife's and leaned over to kiss her.

When they got back to America he would do everything in his power to make sure they had the life that both of them had dreamed of.

CHAPTER NINE

THEY ARRIVED HOME in good time, and the staff met them on the doorstep with huge smiles and welcomes before they hurried to the trunk of their vehicle to remove the suitcases.

Emily stepped through the door of her house and looked at it for the first time as a place she could call *home*. She'd always called it *the house*—never home. But perhaps now it could be? No longer would it be the shell that contained their failing marriage. Now it would be the *home* where she and Sam would be happy. Where they would raise their children and where they would grow old together.

Suddenly the white walls and prestigious art on the walls no longer seemed cold or ostentatious. The place looked inviting, filled with possibilities and hope.

She opened up the French doors out onto the beautiful garden and imagined children chasing each other on the manicured lawns. She could imagine a child marvelling as a butterfly perched on a bloom, or squealing loudly as it ran from a bee. They could have a swing set, a slide, a treehouse put in! They could even get a dog. As a child she'd always wanted one, but Sylvia and Martin had had cats. It was the idea of a dog that warmed her heart. Something large and fluffy with a big pink tongue, that was gentle and kind and would bounce around after her children.

'Doesn't it feel crazy to be back?' she said to Sam, who'd followed her out into the garden.

'A little.'

'We're the ones who have changed and yet it's this place that feels different.'

He looked out across the expanse of grass—at the herb garden, the large Pampas grass, the ornamental bridge. 'Or maybe just our feelings about being in it.'

She looked at him, squinting in the sun. 'What are you going to do now?'

'I'm going to get changed out of these clothes and maybe take a shower. Fancy joining me?'

She laughed and nodded. 'I'll be up in a minute. You get the water running, I just want to have a quick word with Rosie about dinner tonight.'

She wanted to continue their mood from Paris. She wanted to create a beautiful meal for them, to cook him some of his favourites, and she wanted to let the staff know they could have an evening off. Then they would be on their own, and she would arrange a nice romantic table for two, with flowers and candlelight and nice music in the background. There was no need for the romance to disappear just because they'd made it back to reality. She knew, more than anyone, the importance of making time for each other.

She watched Sam head back into the house and then went over to look at the flower garden. There were some pretty blooms there—roses, lilies, aliums. They would be perfect in a little arrangement for the table. She headed back inside to put her plan into action.

Sam trotted upstairs, keen to rid himself of his travel-worn clothes. Nearly twelve hours on a plane, and he'd spilt coffee on his trouser leg. And then, later, as he'd headed to use the bathroom, he'd had a young girl with a sticky lollipop walk into him.

He didn't mind. Accidents happened, and kids always got food on everything. Looking around at their pristine white walls, he smiled as he imagined the housekeepers shooing the children out into the garden so that they didn't get dirty handprints all over the paint.

They'd not had pristine white walls when he was a child. Their rooms had had cheap wood panelling, tough and resistant to handprints and smears. Not to mention the amount of soccer balls that had been accidentally bounced off them.

Soon this house will teem with happy life.

He was proud of himself. Of how far he'd come during their trip. When they'd left for Paris he'd never imagined he would open up the way he had. But he'd not been able to hold it back. All that wonderful time spent with Emily… He'd been so lucky that she had fought for them the way she had. All she'd gone through—the arguments, the accident, his injury, the induced coma, finding out she was pregnant and fearing his reaction—he couldn't imagine he would have been that strong!

Stepping into their bedroom, he began to unbutton his shirt, and as he undid the cuffs he stepped into the en-suite, turned on the shower and checked the water temperature. Perfect. Then he pulled off his shirt and went to put it in the hamper.

He had a small headache. It had been there since about halfway through the flight, and though he'd taken some painkillers he was due for some more. Where would they be?

He checked his bedside drawer, but there was nothing in there save for a book, a packet of gum and a phone charger. Perhaps Emily had some in her bedside drawer? He went over to her side of the bed and pulled it open. There, on top of everything, was a white envelope with his name on it—*Sam*—written in her beautiful familiar handwriting.

Intrigued, he turned it over. It was sealed. But it *was* addressed to him, so he stuck his thumb under the flap and ripped it open, and pulled out the folded piece of paper inside.

He opened it.

Sam,
I'm writing you this letter because I need to. There are things I have to say, to get off my chest, and you're not allowing me the time to sit down and talk to you properly.

You're killing me, Sam. It physically feels like you're ripping out my heart. I never, ever thought that the man who once professed to love me would be able to do this, and hurt me so effectively that I am barely able to function.

All I want is to start a family. Is that so hard? You could have said yes, and everything would have been fine. You could have said no and explained why, but you never do. You never have. Instead you just storm away. Stay away. And whenever you see me in the corridors at work you walk the other way.

Do you have any idea how that makes me feel? How small and how unimportant?

You are my husband, and I love you deeply, but I cannot stay in a relationship that is systematically destroying me.

Once you gave me hope. Now you only cause me pain. I can't live like this any more, and because you won't sit down and talk to me about it I've written this letter instead.

I'm leaving you, Sam. I'm getting out whilst I can, whilst there's still some of 'me' left. I'm not expecting you to come after me. I'm not expecting you to beg me to stay. I don't think you want that at all.

I'm doing this for both of us.

I'm sorry we didn't work out. I'm sorry we're so cut off from each other. I'm sorry to end it this way.

But you never gave me the choice.

Bye, Sam.

Emily

Sam blinked and stared at the words on the page. Was this *real*? It couldn't be! But this was Em's handwriting—he'd recognise it anywhere.

She was leaving me?

He went back to the first page and read it again. He'd not known what to expect when he'd started reading, but he'd never expected a *Dear John* letter.

She was going to leave me...

He frowned and read the words one more time, his heart thudding painfully in his chest.

And then it happened.

A flood of memories came crashing down around him, so fast and so hard he almost went dizzy.

The wedding music as he walked down the aisle with her, looking beautiful in that off-the-shoulder dress...

The honeymoon in Paris, tickling her in bed, hearing her laughter as he turned her to face him and began to kiss her frantically...

Cutting the ribbon to mark the opening of the Monterey, the camera flashes, the cheers, standing in front of the microphone and delivering a speech...

Emily curled up on the couch, her face red with tears, her hand clutching a crumpled white tissue...

Arguing in the car. 'Stop the car! I want to get out!' she'd screamed at him. He'd turned to look at her, there'd been a blare of horns, he'd looked back at the road and...

Sam crumpled the letter in his hand, as his missing years returned with full, brutal force.

* * *

Emily had left instructions for the parts of the plan she'd need help with for Rosie to pass on to the rest of the staff.

'So Paris was wonderful, Mrs Saint?'

'It was the *best,* Rosie—you have no idea.'

'I'm so pleased for you. I know it's been difficult lately.'

Emily thanked her, blushing. She'd forgotten how much the staff must have seen. Heard. Though Rosie might be staff, she was also a good friend, and had often found Emily crying in one of the rooms in the house. She'd always done what she could. Brought her a hot drink. Something sweet and indulgent. Had tried to cheer her. Rosie had stayed late many a night, just to keep Emily company.

'It's all going to be much better from now on.'

'I'm glad.' Rosie shut the fridge. 'I'd already made rosewater pannacotta for your dessert tonight, because they needed to set. Do you still want to have those?'

Emily nodded. 'Sounds delightful. It'll save me some time. I never was any good at desserts—unless I was expected to eat them.'

Rosie laughed. 'That's fine. And I've got some lovely fillet steaks in the fridge—you could do them with a red peppercorn sauce?'

'Thanks, Rosie. Now, I'm going upstairs to wash twelve hours of aeroplane off me. Anything I should know about before I go?'

'No, I don't think so.'

'I'll pick up the correspondence from Sam's desk on my way up—he might want to take a look at that. I know how eager he is to get back to work.'

'Why don't you rest up there for a while? I can bring you up some coffee and cake about three? Would that suit?'

Emily thought that would be perfect. It would give her and Sam plenty of time to be on their own and christen the bedroom with these new versions of Sam and herself.

She left the kitchen quarters and headed up to Sam's office. There was a small pile of mail that had accrued on his desk during their few days away. And she had no doubt that their email accounts would have even more.

But all of that could wait.

She and Sam came first.

She didn't want to go into their bedroom and remind Sam that he had a pile of paperwork waiting for him, but she assumed he must be in the shower already. She could hear the water running.

I'll put it on the bureau.

Emily opened their bedroom door, and then jumped slightly when she saw a figure standing by the bed. 'Oh! Sam! I thought you were in the shower. What are you…?'

She saw his pale face, his stunned expression. Then she saw what he was holding.

A piece of crumpled paper. Her notepaper. And on the bed behind him an envelope, torn along the top, with his name written on it.

The letter.

'Sam—'

'You were *leaving* me?'

She'd never heard him so shocked, so stunned, so hurt, so *appalled*.

Her heart began to hammer in her chest and her mouth went dry as she feverishly began to try to explain. 'Sam, I—'

'You told me countless times that we'd been

arguing. I saw in my own head the memory of our arguing. But you said we were okay.'

'We were…'

'You were going to leave me. You said I was *killing you…*'

'Sam!' Emily couldn't think of what to say. His heartbreak was clear. His devastation was evident. Tears streamed from her eyes when she recalled what she'd put in that letter. She'd been *raw*, she'd been *hurting*, and she'd needed him to know that.

Why hadn't she destroyed that letter?

Because I thought I might have to use it.

She'd not known—could not have predicted—how well things were going to go. Not from the point they'd been at before his amnesia, before their trip to Paris and the strengthening of their love for one another. She hadn't meant for him even to *see* that letter. Not any more! She should have come up here the second they got home and got rid of it. Shredded it. Burnt it.

But she'd forgotten it.

And now he'd read it, and he was hurting and upset. There were even unshed tears in his eyes.

'You wrote this after the accident. You put the date.'

He showed her the letter, but she couldn't look at it. Couldn't face the evidence of her written words.

'You said that our marriage was over.'

'Sam, that was before I knew that you didn't remember. Before I knew that we would get each other back…'

'But you wrote it knowing you were pregnant? Knowing that you'd be walking out on us and leaving our child without its father?'

She heard the hurt, the accusation in his voice. 'Yes, I did. But—'

'You *know* how much I want to be a father, and how much it scares me, *terrifies* me, that I might lose a child—and yet you were willing to walk away from me with our baby?'

Emily hurried to his side, laid a hand upon his arm. 'I didn't know that *then*. All I knew was that you didn't want children! I thought that when I told you in the hospital you would go crazy! Maybe even ask me to get rid of it! I didn't know about Serena!'

'You were going to take my child from me…'

'Sam, that's not fair—'

But he wasn't listening. He dropped the letter and it fluttered to the floor as he stormed from their bedroom and began to run down the stairs.

Emily chased after him and stood at the balustrade, shouting after his disappearing form. 'Where are you going?'

'I'm getting out of here! I need to think!'

She heard the front door slam, the sound echoing through the house, and she stood there, her hands gripping the railings, knuckles gleaming white through her skin, and all she could hear was the sound of the shower running before a car roared into life and she heard the stones sizzle and spit as it roared away down the drive.

She sucked in a big breath and stared into nothing.

What have I done?

Was Sam going to come back? Should he even be driving? He might have an accident. He might get hurt. He…

Emily sank to the floor and rested her head against the stair rail, feeling numb and broken. Her gaze was fixed on the open door.

* * *

He just needed some space. Some air to breathe—air that didn't have Emily in it, complicating matters.

Sam didn't even realise the direction he was travelling. He just drove. Blindly and furiously. His mind going over and over her letter. What it meant. How bad his relationship—his *marriage*—had been.

He never would have imagined he could let it get so bad that his wife would have felt that way. *She said I was killing her...* He swallowed, his throat tight and painful. He shook his head, disbelief filling him. He'd made her feel *that* bad? That was awful. He didn't deserve a woman like that. He didn't deserve all the effort she'd put into him. All the love. Her care. Her attention. That he'd done *that* to her! Made her feel as if she was the last person on earth he'd want to have a baby with…

The baby...

Furiously he wiped at his eyes, desperate to wipe away the stinging sensation burning them. He didn't deserve a child, either.

And suddenly he was at his mom's place. On her driveway. He couldn't remember the journey at all, and as he sat there, blinking, staring at the familiar building where he had spent his childhood, he tried to recall the drive, hoping he hadn't gone through any red lights.

He'd made it here safely, anyway. That was one thing.

But it was strange to be here. He hadn't come back home for over a year. More, he figured, since he'd been married for eighteen months. He'd spoken to his parents on the phone, of course—they'd not been complete strangers—but it had been infrequent and rare. And now he could feel the weight of that guilt upon his shoulders.

Was his mom even in?

His question was answered when she opened the door and peered out to see who had arrived.

She looked the same. A little greyer, maybe, but not much. She still had on those slippers he remembered so well, with the sheepskin inlay. Still seemed to favour those 'mom jeans', with the high elasticated waist, and tucked into them was one of the simple, stripy tee shirts that had always seemed a staple item of her wardrobe.

He stepped out of the vehicle. 'Hi, Mom.'

'Samuel!'

She walked over to him, her arms outstretched, and pulled him into a hug that was as familiar, as comforting, and as painfully heart-warming as he'd remembered them to be.

'Let me look at you! Oh, you look so handsome.'

She smiled as she looked him over, but then, as she gazed carefully at his face, she must have seen, must have sensed something that concerned her.

'What's wrong?'

'Why does something have to be wrong?'

'Because you're home, Samuel, and you swore you would never come back here. Something made you come back. Don't get me wrong—I'm glad. But what is it?'

He hated it that she was so astute. He hated it that he had come here. To this place. To the house that had once held his most painful memory and the people who populated it.

It didn't hold his most painful memory now. Not any more. He had a new pain.

'I just needed to see you, that's all.'

She looked at him sideways, not quite believing him but willing to put it aside for a moment. 'Well, come on in. I'll get you a drink.'

He followed her into the house, sucking in a deep breath before he went through the front door.

It was like stepping back in time. The place looked exactly the same. The same furniture, the same paper on the walls, the same lamps, the same throw rug over the back of the couch. There was even that same old aroma of just-made coffee and freshly baked cookies.

She settled him into a seat and bustled away into the kitchen, making them both coffee and then sitting down with him in the living room.

'How are you feeling after the accident?'

He nodded. 'I'm good.'

'I did visit you. Can you remember?'

'Yeah.'

Of course he remembered. He remembered everything now. All of it. Every hurtful moment.

I can't believe I cut Emily off like that! I walked

away from her when all she needed was an answer from me! I was so angry! So afraid.

He swallowed hard. ‘Do you ever talk about her?’

‘Emily?’ His mom looked confused.

‘Serena.’ He hated having to ask, but he needed to. They’d never mentioned it in this house after she’d died. It was like the elephant in the room.

His mother reached for the necklace at her throat and looked back at him. ‘Why do you ask?’

‘I wonder about it. We never spoke about her. Not after.’

‘Not in the house, no. We chose not to discuss it. You children got so upset.’

‘Not in the house? So you *did* speak about her?’

‘Of course! She was my baby. For a brief time there I thought I might die too, but my pastor helped to get me through.’

‘I didn’t know you were religious.’

‘I’m not. But he met me one day in the supermarket. After the funeral. We began to talk about her and…well, we met every week after that.’

He stared at his mother. ‘Every week?’

She nodded. 'I had to. If I'd kept it inside me, then who knows how I might have ended up.'

He was dumbstruck. All this time! All this time he'd thought it was a forbidden conversation, that no one dared speak her name. And yet all this time his mother had been talking her way through her grief. He was glad. Glad she'd had an outlet. But there was still a question on his mind that haunted him. A question he needed the answer to.

'Did you ever blame me?'

'*You?* Samuel, *no!* Of course not! Why would we? You were a child...you were still in school. It wasn't your fault. It was...' She leaned forward and reached out to lay her hand on his. 'What's going on?'

'I've ruined my marriage.'

She didn't gasp, didn't look shocked—just sat there calmly. 'How?'

'Because of what happened I was afraid to... Emily wanted a baby... No. That's wrong. She wanted to *talk* to me about having a baby and I wouldn't let her.'

'Oh, Samuel...'

'It never occurred to me that as I denied her a

family I was hurting her. I just thought I was protecting myself. I was selfish. The way I treated her…it made her feel as if she were nothing. We kept arguing and I stayed away from home. Stayed away from Em. She was getting ready to leave me when the accident happened.'

His mother sucked in a deep breath. 'I knew she was tense when I saw her in the hospital. I thought she was just worried about you. I never knew any of that was going on.'

'She found out after the accident that she was pregnant. Of course I was in shock. I'd just learnt I'd lost nearly two years of my life and now I was going to be a father? I tried to act pleased. Tried to hide it. The fear, the guilt, eating me away inside.'

He paused.

'We went to Paris to get my memories back. Instead we got close. Closer than we'd ever been before. It was amazing. We shared things. I told her about Serena. She understood where I was coming from. And I finally, *finally* felt like everything was right between us. And then I discovered today, when we got back, that she was going to leave me. Knowing she was pregnant. She was going to walk away. Because of me. Because of how I was with her. I hurt her, Mom. Emotionally. I don't deserve to be with her. With our child…'

She gave him a sympathetic smile. 'I'm going to be a grandmother?'

He nodded. 'Congratulations.'

But he wasn't smiling.

'I don't know what to do. I got my memories back. All of them. I saw what I did. What I *said*. Quite frankly, I'm amazed she stuck around at all.'

'Oh, Samuel, it sounds like she was trying to protect you.'

'Trying to protect herself, more like.'

'I think you're being harsh.'

'I'm not. What if we've always been doomed? We couldn't tell each other basic facts about each other—even after we were married! I had to wait eighteen months before she told me about her childhood, and then I found out that she'd withheld a basic truth from me after we'd promised not to keep anything from each other ever again. We weren't just having the odd argument—we'd been drifting apart for months! We were on the verge of separating.'

He shook his head, still unable to believe how bad things had been.

'I let Paris and our hopes for the trip carry me away. The place wove some sort of magic spell because it had been our honeymoon destination, the city of romance...all of that.'

'Does she still want to leave you now?'

'Probably. After how Dad was I vowed to myself that I would be the best husband there ever could be. I would work hard, but I would be *around*. I'd be home. I'd support my wife, we'd have this great love, this mutual respect—and it turns out I was a huge disappointment. Some of the things I did...said... I was cruel.'

The more he thought about his actions, the more he hated himself. He'd become everything his dad was. Apart from the drinking part. He'd been useless! Distant. Unsupportive. Argumentative. And had he shared with her? No.

He'd let them all down—Emily, Serena, his mom. Himself.

Nobody could be more angry than he felt right now.

His marriage was in tatters.

His mom let out a heavy sigh and reached forward to take both his hands in his. 'Samuel? You deserve to be with Emily. She has *fought* for you! You can't let her down. Not now. Not now you're going to be a father. This isn't just about you any more.'

'Yeah, but—'

'Do you love her?'

He stared at her, saw the intensity in her eyes. 'Of course!'

'Then why are you still here with me?'

Rosie came up the stairs carrying coffee and fresh slices of cake and found Emily sitting on the stairwell.

'Mrs Saint?'

Emily looked up at her with tear-filled eyes.

'Are you okay?' Rosie put down the small tray and hurried over to her employer.

'I think it's all over, Rosie.'

'How? You were just saying earlier how good everything was.'

'He found this.' She pulled the letter from her pocket and passed it over, cringing inwardly as she imagined Rosie's thoughts as she read it. Would Rosie judge her, too?

'Oh…'

'I screwed up. I should have thrown it away. But I forgot it was there. I was just so excited. Sam seemed happy about the baby, we were going on a trip, and I…' She let out a heavy sigh. 'Just as everything was working out right between us. After all those difficulties…you know what I mean. You must have seen. Heard.'

'It was hard not to hear sometimes,' Rosie replied with sadness.

'I'm sorry. You shouldn't have had to hear it at all. We should have sorted it. Been open with each other right from the beginning. We could have avoided this.'

'Mrs Saint, I don't understand everything that's happened, but there is one thing I do know. You and Mr Saint may have had your difficulties, but I have always said that you two were meant for each other. It's not my place to suggest anything, but please don't give up on him. He's a kind man. A good man. This is bound to have shocked him. It would have shocked anyone. Give him time to reflect. Sort things out.'

Emily took back the letter. 'You're very kind,

Rosie, but this is what happens to me. People walk away and leave.'

'You think he's going to walk away?'

'I'm used to it, after my mother… I should have expected it.'

'I'm sure he'll come back.'

Emily looked at her sharply and Rosie quickly stood. 'I've spoken out of turn. I'm sorry. I'll leave you on your own. Call me if you need anything—I'll just be downstairs.'

Rosie hurried away and Emily instantly regretted the sharpness of her gaze. But she hadn't been able to help it. Her first thoughts had run to the fact that he was abandoning her a second time. Her mother had done it once, her husband twice. Was she going to let him do it a third time? A fourth?

It was time to draw a line in the sand.

This wasn't just about her any more. A baby was involved. She'd always vowed that when she had a child of her own it would know love from both its parents. It would grow up in a warm, loving home and would never feel the sting of rejection—certainly not before it was even born!

She was failing her child already.

CHAPTER TEN

'OKAY, SAM. I'M very happy with your progress. You may officially return to work.'

His doctor had given him the good news, expecting Sam to smile.

He hadn't.

He wasn't in a smiling mood.

Sam had spent the last few nights sleeping in his old bedroom at his mother's house, squeezing himself onto a bed that was too small and staring at the ceiling for half of the night. As each morning approached he would resign himself to the fact that he wouldn't get any sleep and then somehow he would, falling into a deep sleep literally an hour or so before he was due to wake up. Then his alarm would blare into his brain and he would jerk awake, bleary-eyed and instantly sad.

He'd not spoken to Emily. He didn't know what to say. How could he go back there? Could he ever say he was sorry enough times? He didn't deserve to be happy with her any more. Surely he'd given up all his chances?

His mother had tried to argue for Emily's side, saying that she must have done what she had to protect him.

Was that true? He tried to imagine himself in her place. Her situation. If it had been Emily in the coma with a brain injury, not him, would he have done the same thing?

Perhaps.

But there was a new equation in all this. The baby. All his life he'd pushed the idea of being a father away. It had been too scary a concept, too terrible even to imagine how that would feel. And because he'd been so busy pushing the idea away, refusing to accept it, he'd never taken a moment to think about whether he really wanted to be a dad.

Hadn't he sworn that he would never be like his own father? So he must have thought about it a little, right? Perhaps it hadn't all been about his guilt over what had happened to Serena? Perhaps his fear had come more from being given the opportunity to have what he wanted most in the world, but then failing miserably? Had it had been easier to lose his temper with Emily and refuse even to talk about having a child than to face up to the possibility that he might fail?

As he drove along the freeway, heading to work, he pondered this. Had it ever really been about Emily? About Serena? Or had it always been about *him*? He was a driven man. He'd provided for his siblings, looked after them, had sent himself to medical school, specialised, set up a thriving business… He'd been successful at everything he'd put his mind to except for what had happened to Serena. He'd failed his sister, and the weight and pain of that failure *haunted* him. Was it that same fear of failure that was driving him now? Having a baby with his wife meant an uncertain future. He couldn't possibly know if he would get it right. Was that why he'd fought against it for so long?

His memories had proved to him that he'd got his marriage wrong once already—did that mean he would continue to get things wrong?

The painful ache in his heart was almost unbearable.

He indicated and pulled over, breathing deeply,

his brain trying to sort through all the memories, putting them in order. He saw them all. The bad. The good. And he remembered their arguments—saw how he had behaved. The words that he'd said. The numerous ways that he had tried to protect himself. He'd not been thinking about Emily! He'd known he was hurting her, had seen how much she wanted a child, but he'd been so concerned about his own vulnerability that he had pushed it back on to her.

He felt sick. Nauseated. He saw over and over again how Emily had kept trying. Trying to talk to him. Trying to find a time that was good for him. Trying to understand why he kept saying no without getting a decent answer from him. He saw how she had begun to retreat from him, hurting and in pain, but how she had still tried. The times he'd come home late and found a table set for two with candles and flowers. The times he'd found her asleep on the couch because she'd been trying to wait up for him.

She fought for us. Despite what I did, she fought for us.

It must have hurt her terribly to consider walking away. To have written that letter.

Sam felt ashamed.

He'd been in the wrong and he'd allowed his fear to keep them apart.

Emily had fought for him. Always. Should he really be giving up on her? Or seeing whether she would give him one last chance? A chance to show her how much he loved *her* and how much he wanted to fight for *her*.

No one had ever fought to stay in her life.

But I'm determined to be the one who does. No matter what.

Desperate to put things right, he picked up his mobile and with trembling fingers called the Monterey.

'It's Sam. Is Emily there today?' He didn't care if the staff were wondering about why he was asking. Surely he should *know* if his wife was working?

'She's at home today, Mr Saint.'

'Thank you.'

He took a deep breath, indicated again, and pulled back out into the traffic. He knew now. He knew what he had to do to put things right.

He was not going to fail at his marriage.

* * *

Emily sucked in a deep breath and closed her eyes as she stood in the garden, the sun shining down upon her face, hoping to find the peace and calm that mindfulness—a technique she sometimes used with her labouring patients—should bring.

It had been an upsetting time since Sam had left, and she'd worried about where he'd gone until she'd received a whispered phone call from his mother to let her know he was safe and well and at her house.

She'd been grateful to his mother for letting her know. It had put her mind at rest.

The garden provided solace. Their private garden, at the back of the house, was in full bloom, populated by some of the flowers that she'd carried in her wedding bouquet—Calla lilies, baby's breath, white roses. They reminded her of that special day they'd had. The day she'd thought all her dreams were coming true.

But the worst had happened. He'd found that awful letter and reacted badly to it. But they could put it right, couldn't they? It didn't have to mean it was the end of everything. No, she hadn't told Sam the whole truth, but she'd been doing it honourably, protecting him from all the harmful things that had been said. Surely he'd be able to see that when he calmed down?

Her cell phone rang in her pocket, disturbing her thoughts.

'Em? It's Sam. I'm coming over.'

She slipped the phone back into her pocket and felt a nervousness start deep down low in her belly. She hadn't expected him to call. He'd said nothing to her for days. Why was he coming? To say goodbye?

Feeling sick, she absently rubbed at her belly.

If he was coming here to say goodbye then she would make sure she told him, one last time, that she had always fought for him, always protected him, always loved him. She would make sure that his last memory of her was one that proved she had never given up on him—even if he was going to try to give up on her.

So she quickly returned to the house, put on the powder-blue dress from Paris. When he arrived she would remind him about their wedding day and remind him of the vows they'd taken. Vows that, to her, had meant everything.

She would not be meek and accept him walking away.

She returned to the garden, seeking that earlier sense of peace she was so desperate to feel again, and waited for him to arrive.

She didn't have to wait long.

She became aware that someone was looking at her, and as she turned back to the house there was Sam, standing on the stone steps leading down to the garden. He had a strange look on his face. He certainly didn't look as angry or as upset as he had the other day, when he had walked away.

Tell him now.

She stepped towards him, but he raised his hand. 'Can I speak first?'

Emily closed her mouth and nodded. She would listen to what he had to say.

'How have you been?'

It wasn't what she'd been expecting. She'd thought he'd come straight out with it. Keep it short. *I'm leaving you for good.*

She refused to cry, but already she could feel tears pressing against her eyes. 'How do you *think* I've been?'

He nodded, his gaze dropping to her belly and then moving up again, to her face. 'I should have told you where I was.'

'You were at your mother's house. She told me.'

'She did?' He seemed surprised, but then he nodded, smiling. 'I should have known.'

'You should have done it yourself.'

He looked right at her, then. 'You're right. I'm sorry.'

Seeing him like this was painful. This man was someone she'd thought she would get to love for ever. Now he was standing across from her like a stranger, and all she could think about was how it felt to be in his loving arms!

'You don't deserve someone like me, Em. Someone who's hurt you like I did. I'm sorry I made you feel that way.'

She sucked in some air. He was building up to it, wasn't he? Why didn't he just say it? Get it out in the open so that she could weep and wail and cry when he was gone?

'Well…'

'Can you give me another chance?'

She stopped breathing. What? What had he just said? She looked up into his face. 'I'm sorry?'

Sam walked up to her. 'I remember.'

Emily frowned. What? He remembered? 'Have you had another memory come back?'

He nodded. 'I've had them *all* come back. I remember it all. The good, the bad. The ugly.'

A small divot formed between her eyebrows.

'I've come here to say I'm sorry. I should never have walked away from you the other day. It was…an old habit. You see, I've learned one or two things since I left. I've realised that most of this—our problems, our disagreements—they were all my fault.'

Really? He was actually saying all these words? Words that meant so much—words that were on the way to healing them. Mending them. Bringing them back together. Was it possible?

Her heart began to pound. But she couldn't let him shoulder all the responsibility.

'No, Sam. It was me. I kept pushing you. Pushing you to commit to a family because I thought if I didn't push you would drift away from me—like everyone else. And you weren't ready.'

'I *was* ready, though. I was just terrified of failing at it.'

She shook her head, not understanding.

'I've always succeeded at everything, but when I lost my baby sister I experienced feelings I didn't know how to deal with. I was sixteen, and no one at home talked about it, so I had to process it myself. Something in me must have decided that I was *never* going to feel that way again. Like I was losing myself. Like I'd lost control. When you asked for a baby that wasn't unreasonable, but I saw it as something I could fail at. I had no certainties, no assurances that everything would be fine and so I pushed it away. Pushed you away. And then I began to fail at my marriage. And though I saw that it was crumbling I tried to pretend that it wasn't happening. I'm sorry.'

'Oh, Sam! I should never have pushed you so hard. There were so many things I'd never been given answers to, and there you were doing it too! I couldn't stand that, when I loved you so much. I still don't know why I was so easy for my mother to leave me behind, but when *you* left me too? I feared there might be something wrong with me. That there was something inherently unloveable about me that made people leave.'

He reached for her hand.

'Or perhaps I pushed them away? I pushed you.'

'No Em. You were never in the wrong. You were—are—incredibly loving and loveable. You didn't push your mother—or me. To me, you said what needed to be said. And I'm glad you did, because it forced me to confront myself. I needed to do that, to see why I behaved like I did, and I'm sorry if I hurt you with anything I have said. I never meant it. I just lashed out verbally because it was easier than dealing with my own issues. I'm sorry, Em. I truly am.'

Emily sank into his arms, her head against his chest. 'Don't be. I trust you, Sam. With my whole heart. I would give it up to you right now.'

They held each other for a moment—a beautiful moment in which the birds sang in the trees around them and the gentle breeze played with the hem of her dress.

'I love you, Sam.'

'I love you, Em.'

They looked at each other, seeing the love they needed, thrived on, lived on. Emily pulled him to her so that her lips could meet his.

The kiss was gentle, solemn, heartfelt. Emily was thrilled that his memories had returned at last, and that he appeared to have worked through his issues. Obviously his time away had helped heal him. If he and his mother had talked about Serena, then hopefully she was healing, too.

When the kiss ended Emily looked up into his eyes and smiled. 'I'd marry you again right now if I could. To prove to you how I feel.'

Sam looked at her and laughed. 'Me too. But, you know, I remember the first lot of vows, and they were pretty damn good.'

'They certainly were.'

He stooped and scooped her up into his arms, and she laughed, surprised.

'Allow me, though, to carry you over the threshold.'

He started heading back towards the house and Emily laid her head against his chest.

This was the dashing Sam she remembered.

The man who'd used to be full of romantic overtures. The gentleman.

The man she loved.

She knew they would be okay now. There was nothing left to break them. No secrets that Sam didn't know. No memories left unremembered.

He knew everything. The good, the bad and the ugly.

Now they could focus on creating more of the good and more of the amazing. She and Sam were united. Husband and wife. Soon to be a family.

The baby would start kicking soon.

And then they would both enjoy their new adventure as parents.

Together.

EPILOGUE

SAM HAD SEEN many babies come into the world, and each of those births had put a smile upon his face. But nothing could have prepared him for the way he felt when his own daughter made it into the world.

Emily had been great. She'd not written a birth plan. She'd just told everyone that she would do what her body told her to do. And when the contractions had got stronger and longer she had chosen to get into the tub.

Her labour had been very relaxed and soothing. Even during the most intense of contractions she had breathed carefully through it, her eyes closed, intent on what was happening within her.

He'd held her hands as she'd got onto her knees in the water. He'd coached her.

'One…two…three…four… And breathe…'

When she'd begun to push the strain on her face had been incredible, but she had borne the pains well and worked with them, using them to help deliver the baby slowly and safely.

As Mia Saint had slithered into the water Emily had gasped and reached down between her legs and brought their daughter to the surface for her first breath.

I'm a father!

She was so beautiful! So perfect!

He hadn't known he could cry so much. He wasn't even aware that tears were pouring down his face until Emily looked up at him with so much love and reached up to wipe them away. He pressed her hand to his face and then kissed her palm, before he laid his hand upon his daughter's head.

No matter what was to come he would protect them both. He would love them to the end of his days. And if there were challenges or difficulties then he knew they would face them together.

These last few months he and Emily had just got stronger and stronger.

He'd delegated, as promised. He'd never worked more than sixty hours a week. And when he was home, he was *present*. Sometimes things didn't get done, but that was okay—because the most important thing was his family.

And now, as he held Mia in his arms, he realised that he was still scared of the responsibility, but he knew in his heart that every father felt the same way. It was natural. Normal.

And, as a father, he knew his daughter would rule his heart.

He would grant her every wish.

If he failed at something, then he would learn from it, and if he needed to lean on Emily then he knew she would be there for him.

He didn't have to do anything alone any more.

He kissed Mia's squashed little nose, then leaned forward and kissed Emily. 'I love you. I'm so proud of you.'

She smiled back and stroked his face. 'And I love you. Don't forget—we're a great team, you and me.'

He kissed her. Slowly. Softly. 'I never forget.'

* * * * *

If you enjoyed this story, check out these other great reads from Louisa Heaton

CHRISTMAS WITH THE SINGLE DAD
SEVEN NIGHTS WITH HER EX
ONE LIFE-CHANGING NIGHT
A FATHER THIS CHRISTMAS?

All available now!

MILLS & BOON®
Large Print Medical

November

Mummy, Nurse...Duchess?	Kate Hardy
Falling for the Foster Mum	Karin Baine
The Doctor and the Princess	Scarlet Wilson
Miracle for the Neurosurgeon	Lynne Marshall
English Rose for the Sicilian Doc	Annie Claydon
Engaged to the Doctor Sheikh	Meredith Webber

December

Healing the Sheikh's Heart	Annie O'Neil
A Life-Saving Reunion	Alison Roberts
The Surgeon's Cinderella	Susan Carlisle
Saved by Doctor Dreamy	Dianne Drake
Pregnant with the Boss's Baby	Sue MacKay
Reunited with His Runaway Doc	Lucy Clark

January

The Surrogate's Unexpected Miracle	Alison Roberts
Convenient Marriage, Surprise Twins	Amy Ruttan
The Doctor's Secret Son	Janice Lynn
Reforming the Playboy	Karin Baine
Their Double Baby Gift	Louisa Heaton
Saving Baby Amy	Annie Claydon

1017 LP 2P P1 Medical

MILLS & BOON®
Large Print Medical

February

Tempted by the Bridesmaid	Annie O'Neil
Claiming His Pregnant Princess	Annie O'Neil
A Miracle for the Baby Doctor	Meredith Webber
Stolen Kisses with Her Boss	Susan Carlisle
Encounter with a Commanding Officer	Charlotte Hawkes
Rebel Doc on Her Doorstep	Lucy Ryder

March

The Doctor's Forbidden Temptation	Tina Beckett
From Passion to Pregnancy	Tina Beckett
The Midwife's Longed-For Baby	Caroline Anderson
One Night That Changed Her Life	Emily Forbes
The Prince's Cinderella Bride	Amalie Berlin
Bride for the Single Dad	Jennifer Taylor

April

Sleigh Ride with the Single Dad	Alison Roberts
A Firefighter in Her Stocking	Janice Lynn
A Christmas Miracle	Amy Andrews
Reunited with Her Surgeon Prince	Marion Lennox
Falling for Her Fake Fiancé	Sue MacKay
The Family She's Longed For	Lucy Clark

017 LP 2P P2 Medical

MILLS & BOON®

Large Print – November 2017

ROMANCE

The Pregnant Kavakos Bride	Sharon Kendrick
The Billionaire's Secret Princess	Caitlin Crews
Sicilian's Baby of Shame	Carol Marinelli
The Secret Kept from the Greek	Susan Stephens
A Ring to Secure His Crown	Kim Lawrence
Wedding Night with Her Enemy	Melanie Milburne
Salazar's One-Night Heir	Jennifer Hayward
The Mysterious Italian Houseguest	Scarlet Wilson
Bound to Her Greek Billionaire	Rebecca Winters
Their Baby Surprise	Katrina Cudmore
The Marriage of Inconvenience	Nina Singh

HISTORICAL

Ruined by the Reckless Viscount	Sophia James
Cinderella and the Duke	Janice Preston
A Warriner to Rescue Her	Virginia Heath
Forbidden Night with the Warrior	Michelle Willingham
The Foundling Bride	Helen Dickson

MEDICAL

Mummy, Nurse...Duchess?	Kate Hardy
Falling for the Foster Mum	Karin Baine
The Doctor and the Princess	Scarlet Wilson
Miracle for the Neurosurgeon	Lynne Marshall
English Rose for the Sicilian Doc	Annie Claydon
Engaged to the Doctor Sheikh	Meredith Webber

1017 GEN STD LP

MILLS & BOON®
Large Print Medical

February

Tempted by the Bridesmaid	Annie O'Neil
Claiming His Pregnant Princess	Annie O'Neil
A Miracle for the Baby Doctor	Meredith Webber
Stolen Kisses with Her Boss	Susan Carlisle
Encounter with a Commanding Officer	Charlotte Hawkes
Rebel Doc on Her Doorstep	Lucy Ryder

March

The Doctor's Forbidden Temptation	Tina Beckett
From Passion to Pregnancy	Tina Beckett
The Midwife's Longed-For Baby	Caroline Anderson
One Night That Changed Her Life	Emily Forbes
The Prince's Cinderella Bride	Amalie Berlin
Bride for the Single Dad	Jennifer Taylor

April

Sleigh Ride with the Single Dad	Alison Roberts
A Firefighter in Her Stocking	Janice Lynn
A Christmas Miracle	Amy Andrews
Reunited with Her Surgeon Prince	Marion Lennox
Falling for Her Fake Fiancé	Sue MacKay
The Family She's Longed For	Lucy Clark

017 LP 2P P2 Medical

MILLS & BOON®

Large Print – November 2017

ROMANCE

The Pregnant Kavakos Bride	Sharon Kendrick
The Billionaire's Secret Princess	Caitlin Crews
Sicilian's Baby of Shame	Carol Marinelli
The Secret Kept from the Greek	Susan Stephens
A Ring to Secure His Crown	Kim Lawrence
Wedding Night with Her Enemy	Melanie Milburne
Salazar's One-Night Heir	Jennifer Hayward
The Mysterious Italian Houseguest	Scarlet Wilson
Bound to Her Greek Billionaire	Rebecca Winters
Their Baby Surprise	Katrina Cudmore
The Marriage of Inconvenience	Nina Singh

HISTORICAL

Ruined by the Reckless Viscount	Sophia James
Cinderella and the Duke	Janice Preston
A Warriner to Rescue Her	Virginia Heath
Forbidden Night with the Warrior	Michelle Willingham
The Foundling Bride	Helen Dickson

MEDICAL

Mummy, Nurse...Duchess?	Kate Hardy
Falling for the Foster Mum	Karin Baine
The Doctor and the Princess	Scarlet Wilson
Miracle for the Neurosurgeon	Lynne Marshall
English Rose for the Sicilian Doc	Annie Claydon
Engaged to the Doctor Sheikh	Meredith Webber

1017 GEN STD LP